THE FATHER AND THE FOREIGNER

Giancarlo De Cataldo

THE FATHER AND
THE FOREIGNER

*Translated from the Italian
by Ann Goldstein*

Europa
editions

Europa Editions
116 East 16th Street
New York, N.Y. 10003
www.europaeditions.com
info@europaeditions.com

Copyright © 2004 by Edizioni e/o
First Publication 2009 by Europa Editions

Translation by Ann Goldstein
Original Title: *Il padre e lo straniero*

Library of Congress Cataloging in Publication Data is available
ISBN 978-1-933372-72-3

De Cataldo, Giancarlo
The Father and the Foreigner

Book design by Emanuele Ragnisco
www.mekkanografici.com

Prepress by Plan.ed – Rome

Printed in Canada

THE FATHER AND THE FOREIGNER

For Francesca,
who is no longer here

Chapter 1

D iego was smoking a cigarette. It was ten minutes before the end of the session. A cool autumn breeze was blowing, and, in the middle of the grassless patch of ground that separated the convulsives' unit from the brain-damaged unit, some epileptic children were playing tag under the distracted gaze of an old woman intent on her knitting. Two therapists were trying to hold up a child with a tiny head. Diego had already noticed that small, disjointed creature, who seemed a freak of nature. To himself he called him "the little monster."

He didn't see the man until he sat down next to him, on the shady side of the bench. He was tall and olive-skinned, in his forties, with deep black eyes and an elegance that bordered on affectation. Diego stared obstinately at the tips of his shoes.

Usually, the parents exchanged a nod of greeting or some comment on the weather or the children. Diego had never allowed himself the solace of talking. What help would there be in the complaints or advice of others? There had been a time when he felt ashamed of the catastrophe that had befallen him. In the end he had convinced himself that in grief, as in rage, one is always alone and powerless.

The man had begun tapping his foot, obsessively. Suddenly he let out a deep sigh. Diego was surprised to find that in spite of himself he was looking at him. The other intercepted his gaze and gave him a gentle smile.

"You, too, are here for a child?"

He spoke the words calmly, stressing the accents heavily. The inflection was unclear, definitely foreign, maybe Middle Eastern, to judge from the olive complexion and the shadow of a beard that seemed to challenge even the most diligent shaving. Diego, too, sighed, and nodded.

"In this season, in my country, in the villages below the heights, there's a big celebration. We dance to keep away the fear of winter. My name is Walid."

Diego shook the hand that the other held out, and muttered a "Diego Marini" that made him feel ridiculous and at the same time infuriated him. "What is your country?" he added immediately.

"Oh, it's far away. But not that different from Italy. We, too, have the mountains and the sea, and all types of people. We of the coast say that those in the mountains don't wash, because it's cold. Those from the mountains say that we of the coast stink of fish. That's my son, Yusuf."

So he was the father of the "little monster." Strange, though, he so dark and that child with a tuft of fair hair . . .

Then Diego thought again of the tone in which the man had pronounced the child's name: with pride and sorrow. His wife had often reproached him for this, for never having learned to say his child's name with equal pride and sorrow.

"Mine is still inside," he murmured, standing up suddenly. "It's time for me to get him."

When he entered the therapy room, the girls had

already dressed Giacomo and a mother was impatiently waiting her turn, hugging a small red-cheeked child, whose tongue was tirelessly exploring the roof of her mouth.

Diego leaned over to whisper something in his son's ear. The child's face was illuminated by a radiant smile, and he let out his cry of happiness, an *eeeh-eeeh*, monotone and modulated at the same time, thanking his father for freeing him from the therapists.

For Giacomo every session was torture: but, according to the doctors, this torture was necessary for the development of his malformed brain. After two years of assiduous therapy, he had learned to smile at his parents and prop up his pacifier with the back of his hand. He could stand, if supported, for thirty seconds. Diego was sure now that he was resigned to Giacomo's illness: but when, some days, at home, he felt a breath of vague optimism for the child's "progress," he was overcome by a fierce burst of rage. All that struggle seemed to him useless or, worse, an absurd violence. If he had been something more than a lowly employee at the Ministry of Justice, he would have said of himself that, with the birth of his son, he had died inside.

In the courtyard he saw Walid again: dancing in the middle of it as he hugged the little monster. The child's head hung to one side, his eyes were empty, but on his lips hovered the same smile as his father's.

They found themselves side by side, pushing their strollers, as they walked along the path that led to the entrance of the institute. Arriving at the glass door that opened onto an avenue clogged with traffic, they stopped to adjust the children. Giacomo was still smiling, a thread of saliva in the corner of his chapped mouth. Yusuf had fallen asleep.

They exchanged a nod of farewell. The gentle smile reappeared on Walid's face, then he set off toward a long black limousine parked in front of the institute. A Middle Eastern man in a chauffeur's uniform got out of the driver's seat, bowed to Walid, and helped him lift the child.

As he headed for his own beat-up Panda, Diego thought he would like to see that serene father again. And he was deeply ashamed of having thought of Yusuf as the "little monster."

Chapter 2

Diego had seen the first handicapped child of his life thirty-two years earlier, on the steps of the Mazzini middle school. It was a rainy day, and school was letting out, the children swarming toward freedom. The child was clutching his mother and furiously scratching one ear, both of them, mother and son, hunched over in identical dull gray jackets. Meeting the boy's vacant gaze as he passed by, Diego had been unable to repress a shudder. Although he was only eleven, that fleeting vision had tormented him for a long time, to the point where he felt impelled to talk to his parents about it. His mother had told him that it was only an unfortunate child, his father that certain spectacles should be kept at home, and the matter ended there.

A few years later, as a teenager, he had been beaten at ping-pong by a skinny kid who held the racquet in his left hand and had an empty sleeve in place of his right arm. Curious, he had asked the boy to show him what was inside the sleeve. The other had readily shown him a kind of partridge wing, mentioning something about a drug with an odd name, Thalidomide. That night Diego went home filled with shame for the surge of disgust he had been unable to hide.

The third handicapped child of his life was his son, Giacomo. He was born on a Saturday morning, and as soon as the doctors pulled him out of Elsa's womb, and showed him, small and bluish, wrinkled and silent, to Diego, he had felt an inexplicable repulsion. It took at least five minutes for Giacomo to make his voice heard, a weak, intermittent bleat, the lament of a creature that it was not right to bring into the world.

Diego had broken down in tears, a reaction that was attributed to the emotion of his new fatherhood. Elsa's tears came later, when more exact diagnoses confirmed the suspicions of the family pediatrician: but for a long time Diego believed he had already spent his own grief in that first, premonitory outburst.

As he was telling all this to Walid, he realized that he had never talked about it with anyone before. It had been almost three years, and only with this stranger had he found the courage to open up. Diego brought Giacomo to therapy every Saturday, his free day. It was the third Saturday they'd met, and Walid had proposed that they use the familiar *tu*. They were sitting at a table in a café opposite a row of buildings that included a squalid parking garage, some marble-cutting workshops that specialized in gravestones destined for the nearby cemetery, and a cheap wine store, the walls decorated with red and black graffiti. At the table next to theirs three workers in overalls were cursing the government and their unemployment benefits. Walid finished sipping his coffee, which he had diluted with hot water, and pointed to the graffiti.

"That one is against the Islamic government of Iran," he said, in an Italian that resonated more of grammatical study than of the habit of conversation. "Near my house there are graffiti saying 'God exists.' They seem to be the work of a madman."

"Maybe it's God himself," Diego murmured.

"If he exists he must be very angry with us. But if he is so angry that now and again, to get revenge, he randomly strikes someone, maybe an innocent person, then I prefer to believe that he doesn't exist. In my country many believe in Allah and some in Jesus Christ. Even that is a fact that I don't find compelling. All believers say that there is one God. And naturally it is their God. But if there is only one God, what importance does his name have? Each of us can give him the name he prefers, don't you think?"

"I don't know. When I was very young I went to church, like everyone else. And I made my first communion and even confirmation. I had a church wedding. I've always done what everyone else does."

Walid was silent. They focused on the street again: Housewives weighed down by bags with bunches of celery and long loaves of bread sticking out of them. A nurse in a white jacket, dragging an epileptic boy of about thirteen, for Diego the "wolf-boy," because of his hunched shoulders, the cries that sometimes convulsed his jaws, his improbably elongated head, the mass of curls that, from his hair to his premature beard, formed an inextricable whole, a grotesque mane.

A high-school girl went by in a miniskirt and a white shirt that let her exuberant breasts bounce joyfully in the sun. They followed her with their eyes, exchanging a mute nod of appreciation. Walid smiled.

"The night Yusuf was born, I dreamed that many friends came bearing crowns and they said that he would become the king of his people. And the next morning, when the doctors informed me that there were some problems, I wept. You were more fortunate, my friend, because your tears came from the heart. Mine came from the brain. You understood before you knew. I needed to be told by others."

"I don't think that's true," Diego murmured.

Walid said he had read in a book that the problem for their children was the nonexistence of the outside world.

"We have to push the world toward them. We have to learn to think in a different way. Otherwise, the grief kills."

Each paid for himself and then they returned to the institute to pick up the children. Before saying goodbye, Walid told Diego to blow on Giacomo's face.

"It's an experiment that psychologists have tried. If you blow on your child's face, and he laughs, it means he's loved. If he cries, it means he's not loved enough."

Diego blew hard on Giacomo's cheeks, which the child let him do, first surprised, then interested, until he decided that he had had enough and turned away without a complaint or a smile.

Chapter 3

Toward the end of November, the two fathers went shopping in the market in Piazza Vittorio. Walid had insisted that they take his car. Diego noticed that his friend had a number of permits for places normally off-limits to cars.

"Are you a diplomat?"

"Something like that," he answered, and the matter ended there.

Their Saturday meetings had become a habit that at this point neither would have been able to give up. Each time the conversation touched on some detail of Walid's private life, he tended to gloss over it, and while by now very little about the modest emotions and many disappointments of Diego Marini was unknown to his secret companion, Diego knew almost nothing about him, not even his surname—assuming that his country, which was also shrouded in mystery, used surnames. But it wasn't important to Diego. He had never felt so in tune with anyone, not even his wife.

After that first encounter at the institute, he had felt explosions of tenderness for Giacomo that took him by surprise, hitting him with the strange force of a troubled joy. But since that morning at the café, neither he nor Walid, through a tacit understanding, had spoken of their children and their fate.

The chauffeur maneuvered skillfully, and the big sedan wedged itself between the cars double-parked near Porta Santa. A scowling traffic cop observed the stickers on the car with impotent rage and turned to look elsewhere. Walid gave the driver a brief order in Arabic, and, together with Diego, plunged into the throug of the market.

"Here's a place where even a foreigner feels at home." And he led Diego into the Arab section, where, with increasing curiosity, Diego watched Walid's extensive bargaining. The neighborhood residents had always been on a war footing with the casbah of immigrants who had transplanted their incomprehensible customs and suspect goods into the heart of the most ancient city in the West. In popular fantasies and resentments, painted Gypsies, clever Moroccans, dignified Indians, chattering South Americans, pallid Poles, and very black Equatorial Africans were only a single undifferentiated personification of the Different Foreigner. These strangers came to take away their jobs; they raped their women, kidnapped their children, stole, sold drugs on street corners, carried diseases, and lived in filth. They were hated. They had turned Italy into a racist country.

Diego didn't have clear ideas on the subject, or on politics, or religion, or any other subject. But of one thing he was certain: Walid did not belong to that ragged throng elbowing in to grab a kilo of rotten greens or a live chicken. Like everyone else, Diego shooed away the windshield cleaners who pestered him at traffic lights; very occasionally, he gave them a coin: it depended on chance, on mood, on how much of a hurry he was in. But the windshield cleaners, like the people who sold cigarettes or matches, were beggars; Walid was a friend.

Suddenly Walid had vanished. And yet only a moment earlier he had been arguing furiously with a spice vendor . . . Diego felt alone in the midst of a hostile crowd, alone with his half kilo of salmon in a plastic bag in one hand, tomatoes and oranges in the other. Was that how the others felt, the foreigners? Walid didn't seem to feel uneasy in Italy. On the contrary, Diego realized with a certain obscure fear, he felt out of place without Walid. He headed toward the car; the driver, surprised to see him appear alone, said something in Arabic and picked up the cigarette he had thrown on the ground. Walid appeared a few minutes later, loaded down with packages and bags. From one of the bags the long ears of a lamb were sticking out.

"We're late, friend. The children are waiting," and he ordered the driver to take them back to the institute.

"What are you doing this afternoon?"

Diego said that he had planned to visit his family.

"Too bad, I wanted to take you to Mustafa's. Mustafa is Turkish, and that in general is a flaw, but Mustafa is a friend, and that is always a good thing. Mustafa has the most Turkish Turkish baths in all of Europe. And after the massage you can eat real kebab, and drink real Turkish coffee. The Turks are not people you can trust, but their coffee never lies!"

"I can try to get out of it . . . "

"I'll pick you up around seven."

"But didn't you say afternoon?"

"You Europeans! In my country the afternoon begins at seven."

"And what about night, when does that begin?"

Walid smiled mysteriously. "The night always holds some surprises!"

When, exactly at seven, Walid rang the bell, Diego realized that he had never told him where he lived. And he went down to meet his friend with a certain uneasiness.

Chapter 4

The Turkish baths were a few meters from the old day hotel on Via Cavour. There was no sign; only, at the top of three steps, an old man in a turban with a towel over his arm. Mustafa was a fat Turk, sweaty and smiling. He embraced Walid again and again, exchanged a vigorous handshake with Diego, and finally entrusted them to the care of a wiry teenager with a sad look on his face. The two friends took off their clothes in a wood-paneled dressing room, and the boy led them into the bath. The steam grabbed Diego by the throat. He felt faint, and only after Walid had sat him down on a burning-hot marble bench could he distinguish anything in the vaporous air. He saw crumbling walls dripping with dampness and shapeless silhouettes converging on a large pool. Walid told him to follow, and Diego took some steps in the direction of the pool, but when it was his turn to go in he felt strangely afraid. Several times he shook his head no and gripped the railing, and he stood there, motionless, until Walid gave him a sharp push that sent him tumbling into the water. A few minutes later, sitting on the bench again, he thanked his friend for that energetic treatment.

"It's always like that the first time. You have to plunge in, my friend. The secret of the Turkish bath is this: half water and half sweat. Which is the same thing, all water. In my country, bigoted people say that the Turkish bath distances you from God, because it mixes spirit and flesh. But I say that something so beautiful can do no wrong to God. And naturally the Turkish bath isn't complete without a good massage."

The teenager, who had evidently been assigned to them, smiled and said something in Arabic. Walid answered, then the two of them laughed, pointing to Diego. Walid reassured him:

"Tariq is the best masseur in Rome. Even though he looks so thin, he has fingers of steel. He looks like a boy, but he's forty-two. He's a real artist of the body. He says you have no respect for your body, but if you'll entrust yourself to him for one month, he'll make you muscular and flexible, like a real man!"

They laughed. They went back into the pool. They talked. They bathed yet again. The time passed unnoticed, just slipping away. When Tariq informed them that it was time for the massage, Diego endured the ritual with resignation and not a single complaint. He discovered that he had creaking bones and tissues that groaned desperately under the pressure of Tariq's fingers, and when, finally, Mustafa served them, in large silver cups, a rich-smelling black syrup, Diego felt pure and light as an angel.

Later, in Mustafa's small office, while Tariq kept pouring cool water from hand-painted potbellied carafes, Walid and the Turk began to talk animatedly in a harsh, guttural language. A shifty-looking attendant entered and whispered something in Walid's ear. Walid went off with him. Mustafa took a big hookah with six openings from a dark wood cabinet, quickly wiped clean the little bowl, put in four or five chunks of something compact and black, lit them, offered a hose to Diego. He inhaled, but nothing happened. Mustafa smiled.

"Not so soft, friend. Very, very hard!"

Diego breathed in with all the strength he had in his body. The water in the glass bowl boiled furiously, and something violent struck him in the pit of his stomach, cutting off his breath.

"It's too strong for me," he said, coughing, and was about to give the hose back to Mustafa.

"No, no! Walid will be offended if you don't smoke with him! You're the first Italian he's brought here. That means he is your true friend. And Walid's friendship is something serious. Walid is a very important man. Try again. Not so gentle as the first time, not so strong as the second! The right way, friend. Sooner or later everyone finds the right way!"

Diego found his on the fourth attempt. The smoke was thick and sweetish, and as it traveled through his lungs it produced a stupor to which he abandoned himself with pleasure.

"Who is Walid really? What does he do?"

"You don't know? Oh, well, then I can't say. I can't tell you if Walid doesn't want to tell you himself first. Do you tell one friend's secrets to another? It's not right. Women tell secrets. Not men!" Tariq nodded gravely.

Diego felt that between these men there was a bond so strong and enduring it could be identified with their very lives. He wished ardently to share it, and wondered what he could to be admitted among them. He wanted to be their equal.

"Anyway," Mustafa added, smiling suggestively, "Walid does many things, and all of them are important."

At that moment his friend returned. He uttered a brief phrase, and suddenly the atmosphere in the room changed. Tariq left without a word, Mustafa banged a fist on the table. Then they both stared at Diego.

"I have to go, on some urgent business," Walid said, "but you can stay with Mustafa."

Mustafa nodded, not too eagerly. Diego rose, swaying. "I think I'll go home, Walid."

"I'm sorry, I can't take you. Mustafa will call you a taxi."

They shook hands. Walid was visibly upset and preoccupied.

"Can I do something to . . . "

"Oh, it's nothing, but I have to be there," Walid reassured him, and then, still gripping his hand, and staring straight into his eyes, he said, "Stay close to your son, my friend."

Chapter 5

A little before the Christmas vacation, Walid showed up at the institute in the company of a tall, slender woman, her large Oriental eyes emphasized by clever makeup. Under a gray coat one could divine a suit of an austere cut, of the type worn by PR agents or airplane hostesses. Walid said to Diego that Zaira was his oldest friend, and to Zaira that Diego was his newest friend.

"I thought it was right for you to meet. And also I wanted to show Zaira a place I'm very fond of."

Diego shook her hand, which was soft, the fingers covered with rings, and felt that he didn't like this woman. He couldn't say precisely what wasn't right about her, but he didn't like her.

As he observed her—hips swaying as she walked, slim and perhaps unconsciously enticing—Diego wondered if she was only a friend. He also wondered if she was possibly Yusuf's mother, but the thought seemed to him, for some inexplicable reason, irreverent. He and Walid had never talked about their wives. He wasn't even sure that his friend had a wife. There were many other things they had never talked about. Nor had Walid ever let slip the slightest allusion to the evening at the Turkish baths, and he, out of discretion, had not asked him the reason for that abrupt departure.

"Here, it's here."

So, he had brought her to billiards! They went in and asked the owner to prepare their regular table. Diego had introduced his friend to the place, an old movie theater converted to a pool hall. They had spent a couple of mornings challenging each other at carambole, his favorite game. The place was big, cool, immersed in a friendly half-light. Usually at that hour of the morning they were the only players; it might be said that the manager was there just for them. It was nice to be silent as the game proceeded, breathing in the odor of sweat and smoke that hovered in the room, to let one's gaze wander among the unused billiard tables dozing under their green cloths, light a cigarette or drink a Coke, approve with a nod a well-placed shot, pass the blue chalk over the point of the cue, adjust the score. It was as if they were lords of a solid world, without unexpected events, from which fear and sorrow had been banished.

Without consulting him, Walid had decided to introduce that woman into their billiard game. And Diego, confused, felt her appearance as an intrusion into their friendship. That was what was wrong with Zaira: she was invading the territory of Saturdays that belonged to fathers who were no longer solitary.

The manager announced that their table was ready. Walid and Zaira took cues from the rack and arranged the balls and the cue ball.

"We'll start," Walid said, "since you're the best. The winner will challenge you."

For a while Diego followed the game distractedly. Then, making some excuse, he left. Their Saturday was over, by now. He had almost reached the institute when he decided to go back. Why offend Walid so stupidly? But when he returned to the pool hall, his friend was gone. And Zaira held out the cue to him with an indecipherable smile.

It had stopped raining, but it was cold. The passersby stiffly pulled their coats tight and raised the collars to protect themselves from a gusty wind that had the scent of a storm. Zaira took him familiarly by the arm, and Diego started at the pressure of her fingers. She seemed to lean on him with a kind of abandon. Diego felt relieved when they sat down at a table in the usual café.

They ordered aperitifs. Zaira rummaged in her purse, took out a long thin cigarette, and lit it.

"Is this where you come with Walid?" she asked, resting a hand on his arm. Diego nodded. She spoke the same formally correct but unidiomatic Italian as Walid.

"Walid often speaks of you. He was very sad before he met you."

"That happens to fathers," Diego said, curtly.

The aperitifs came. The woman drank hers in a single gulp, avidly. She took one of Diego's hands between hers, turned it so as to frame the palm.

"This is the life line. This other is the line of fortune. This . . . "

Diego withdrew his hand abruptly and made a move to stand up.

"I have to go. The child . . . "

"Wait!"

It was an invocation, a call for help or perhaps an order. Diego stopped, puzzled. The woman was dangerously close to him.

"I want to tell you something," she whispered. "Walid

says that children like Yusuf need two fathers, because one isn't enough for someone so defenseless. He is your friend, and he is also the father of your son. And you are his friend and you are also the father of Yusuf. So he will be at your side when you need him. But don't tell him that I told you this."

He left her sitting at the table, and forgot to pay for his drink. Giacomino, cheerfully prattling, dragged a smile out of him, in which, again, the old disappointment and bitterness surfaced. At the institute they told him that Yusuf had left half an hour earlier. With his father.

Chapter 6

The following Friday, Walid telephoned him at the office.

"I won't be there tomorrow. I'm going on vacation, my friend. But first we're having a kind of party. You'll come, of course."

"A party? When?"

"Tonight. And this time it goes all night: no joke."

"At your house?"

"At a club, the Arabesque. I'll pick you up at nine."

"Jacket and tie?"

"What?"

"Do I need to wear a jacket and tie?"

"You can come naked. It's a private party. Only good friends."

"All right. At nine, then."

A tense afternoon followed: the child was agitated, and refused to sleep, nor would he calm down in the stroller; if he was put in the special orthopedic chair that was supposed to teach him to hold his back erect, he tended to slump, sliding to one side and crying inconsolably. Diego and his wife were forced to take turns holding him. Diego didn't know how to explain his going out in the evening. He hadn't yet told her about Walid. It was something too much his own. He didn't want to share with her that privileged space. For the same reason he had been bothered by the intrusion of Zaira. Out of jealousy. No one else was supposed to set foot in that space for two. Elsa wouldn't understand. And a frank explanation would wound her.

At eight-thirty he took a shower, put on a suit and his best overcoat, and simply went out the door, informing his wife that he would be home late.

He waited for ten minutes in the street, smoking, until he saw a large car with foreign plates. Walid sounded the horn and he got in. As always, his friend looked elegant, and seemed in good form, even euphoric.

"You'll see, it's going to be a great party!"

"I don't know if this was a good idea, Walid."

"Your wife objected?"

"It's not just Elsa. It's that in certain situations I don't feel comfortable."

Diego confided to Walid the unease he had always felt in discothèques, piano bars, night clubs. He had been like that even as a student, when he and his friends went in a group to pick up mythical girls. For him there were only the parties at home on Saturday afternoons—that was the only time he managed to feel some trace of erotic vibration toward the more attractive schoolmates, or at least the less disdainful. The occasions, and they were not many, when Elsa or some friend had insisted on taking him dancing, he had felt apprehensive. All that noise and confusion made him sad, and, as for the people who seemed to be enjoying themselves so much, he thought that, basically, it was nothing but a multitude of solitudes bound together by the common celebration of rites whose meanings and whose codes escaped him.

"This time will be different, you'll see."

They were far out on the Cassia, where the urban periphery dissolved into open country. Walid parked in an unpaved lot, crowded with big cars guarded by uniformed drivers, and led him to a one-story building. There was a row of lowered metal shutters and an armored door with a microscopic nameplate: "Arabesque—Private Club." Walid rapped with his knuckles. Two dark examining eyes appeared at a peephole, then the door was flung open. A man with a ponytail threw himself at Walid and embraced him three times.

Walid took off his expensive, tailor-made overcoat and handed it to the man with the ponytail. Diego did the same.

"That's Michel," Walid said, as they descended a steep staircase, "the manager. He's half Armenian and half Greek."

Their goal was a close, dark cellar. Seven or eight small tables, divided from one another by alcoves dug into the wall, surrounded an empty dance floor. On the left was a bar and, beside it, a narrow stage barely large enough to hold a small electric piano.

A dozen or so people stood idly at the bar, mostly middle-aged men in gaudy jackets and buxom women dripping with brilliant jewels. Real or fake: Diego would have liked to know. Though, after all, what difference did it make? Walid headed for the bar, calling someone loudly. His appearance electrified the crowd. Men and women fell on him, some embraced him, some seized his hand in an exaggerated grip, and more than one look of approval came to rest on Diego, who stood a few steps behind, overcome by his usual discothèque embarrassment.

Finally, the greetings over, Walid clapped his hands.

The room grew quiet, and a beam of light framed the stage around the piano. A young man with slicked-back hair settled himself at the instrument and immediately a sentimental-sounding singsong melody started up that was welcomed warmly by the onlookers. Walid, holding two glasses filled with an amber liquid, returned to Diego, and guided him to a table next to the musician.

They sat down. Diego tasted the drink. It was a strong, aromatic tea, with a hint of peaches or some tropical fruit.

"I thought night clubs served stronger stuff, Walid."

"Some of my friends are believers in the true faith. Matter of form. Believers are very sensitive. And they don't drink alcohol. But, if you prefer, you can order champagne."

"This is fine. What's this whining all about?"

"What do you mean whining! It's one of the most beautiful songs of my country. He's saying that he's very sad because his woman has left him and run away with a tall blond sailor. One assumes that he is small and dark."

"A sad story."

"Wait. Now he says, All right, you're gone, but I can find a hundred better than you. And I want them all tall and blond."

The final notes of the song were uttered in chorus by the audience, which then rewarded the singer with enthusiastic applause. The man thanked them and announced the next piece, which to Diego seemed similar in every respect to the first.

This time, however, everyone began dancing. Men and women: a strange dance, with languid, sensual movements. From the dance floor, someone gestured broadly at Walid, but he shook his head. A waiter brought two plates to their table.

"Couscous, of course."

Diego had never tasted couscous, and he liked it. In the meantime, the place was filling up, and all of the arrivals, fat Arab men, with women covered in gold, came by to pay their respects to Walid and shake Diego's hand.

"There!" Walid exclaimed, pointing to a rather fleshy woman who was wearing an outfit of embroidered black veils. "That's Jamira."

The musician stopped and a murmur spread through the room. Jamira stopped by Walid's table and bowed. Walid got up and kissed her hand. The onlookers applauded. The musician started an even more plaintive singsong. Jamira went to the center of the dance floor. The murmuring ceased.

"She's the greatest belly dancer in the world," whispered Walid.

Jamira began her number. On her arms and feet and around her stomach she wore rings and curious castanets that jingled to the rhythm of her movements.

"Isn't she amazing?"

Diego nodded politely, not entirely convinced.

"You're thinking she's fat," Walid said softly. "But it's not like that. In belly dancing you have to see the movement of the flesh around the belly button. There's nothing more exciting than that wriggling around the small, exposed hole . . . Look, look how she bends her knees . . ."

The woman's forehead was beaded with sweat, and a dark liquid was dripping from the edges of her heavy makeup. The music became obsessive, insistent. Now Jamira was completely stretched out on the floor, in an unnatural position, and all the energy of her body seemed to be concentrated in the jingling of the rings around her stomach. Walid got up and went over to her. Everyone began to clap rhythmically. Walid leaned over her, and she stretched up toward him. In a slow, maddening movement, the woman began to rise, inch by inch, while Walid, on his knees, retreated before her. Diego cast a panoramic glance: dozens of eyes were following the scene with hypnotic attention. Foreheads bathed in sweat, eyes sparkling with passion. The men grabbed their women, touched them, and they yielded, without taking their gaze from the dancers. Now Jamira was half-erect, and, using her legs as a lever, was rising up completely; Walid, at her feet, continued to lower himself as his shoulders rotated. The singsong, violent and seductive, was marking time. Diego felt himself captured by a magic flow: the two weren't even touching, but how could you not read in their moves an explicit sexual reference . . . Abruptly, Jamira stood up and pushed Walid away from her with an imperious arm gesture. The music died in an extreme, prolonged suffering note. He fell to the floor. The lights went on. He got up. For an instant, an unreal silence reigned in the room. Then a liberating applause broke out. Walid embraced Jamira; panting and sweaty, she bowed to the audience. The lights dimmed. Walid went back to the table.

"Still uncomfortable?"

Diego shook his head no vigorously. Walid smiled, but in his bright eyes there were depths of despair. Diego shivered.

"She really was dancing for you?"

"In my honor. Jamira came from Algeria just to dance in my honor!"

There was a strange contrast between the pride with which he uttered these words and the sorrow that he seemed to want to communicate. It was as if pride and sorrow were battling one another . . .

"What is it that you're celebrating?"

Walid didn't answer. He shook his friend's hands hard, and on his lips the usual gentle, indecipherable smile reappeared.

"You Westerners! You always put everything into your compartments! Who said it's a celebration? For you, when it's a celebration it's a celebration. And that's it. When it's work, it's work. And that's it. When it's sorrow, it's sorrow. For us, on the other hand, celebration, work, sorrow are all one thing. So when men work too much or suffer too much, that calls for a good party. In my country, when someone dies, we all gather, friends and relatives of the dead man, and have a big party. The dead man is in the other room, and you have to make a lot of noise, so he doesn't hear the great silence and think that everyone's already forgotten him. We eat, we drink, and we dance until we fall fainting under the table, and those who have any strength left carry off those who can't make it. And the next day we begin again with new work, a new sorrow, and a new party!"

"It was you who told me it was a celebration!" Diego protested. Walid smiled.

"But it is a celebration! And now, to make it complete, it's your turn."

Jamira, appearing out of nowhere, grabbed him by the hands, dragging him toward the dance floor. All the guests arranged themselves around the space reserved for the dancing. Diego sketched a desperate gesture of denial, but he felt the weight of encouraging eyes on him. The music began, livelier this time, it seemed, or maybe he was beginning to get used to those strange rhythms.

"Let yourself be led," Jamira whispered. He glanced at Walid. His friend was sipping his tea, lost in the depths of his glass, and to Diego it seemed that he was crying. He let himself go, and he discovered that his body could be forced to draw geometries that he would never have believed himself capable of, and he sank into the scent of the dancer, her wild, heavy perfume. Out of the corner of his eye he saw that the circle around them was narrowing, and he could feel her body, he felt it without even being touched by it, and it was as if they were at opposite ends of a rope that vibrated with the movement of their flesh, and finally he found himself stretched out, animated by a shaking that it was impossible to control, until the last note arrived, the lights, the applause, hands that lifted him bodily, and cries of triumph.

When he returned to the table—they'd made him drink something strong, at the bar; after all, he was allowed, and he had downed one, two three glasses, dispensing smiles and even receiving wet kisses from the robust women— Walid wasn't there. In his place was Michel, the manager.

"He left on urgent business, but he'll be back right away. I'm supposed to take care of you."

He spoke with a slight French accent, he might be thirty-five, his face marked by a professional tan, deep circles under his eyes.

"You command and I obey, boss! Do you like my place? This is a special evening. Only friends. A lot of people, very well known. No strangers. You command and I obey, boss!"

Diego seemed to detect a slight sarcasm in Michel's voice. But maybe he was only trying to be nice.

"Nothing, thank you. I still have to recover . . . "

"You're very lucky to be a friend of Walid's. Walid's friendship has great weight in our circle."

Michel told him that for that evening, and forever, he was to consider himself a welcome guest of the Arabesque. Diego stopped a waiter and offered to buy him a drink.

Michel ordered two gin and tonics.

"We're not Arabs, the two of us!" he whispered, with satisfaction.

The club was overflowing. The pianist had yielded his place to a disk jockey, who dispensed a more digestible rock. Michel continued to talk and talk, but Diego wasn't listening to him. He had made out Walid. He was at the back of the bar, engaged in close conversation with a European in a dark suit, a man in his fifties, rather short, grizzled, whose sober elegance stood out amid the shiny vulgarity of the other guests. The conversation must be very serious, demanding. Walid had a dark expression that Diego didn't like; he imagined that the other was saying something unpleasant, that the two were near quarreling. Even less did he like the cruel line of the man's mouth, his gaze that looked insincere, indirect, and for some reason, it occurred to him, treacherous.

Michel was saying something about a message.

"What message, I'm sorry?"

"I was saying that, unfortunately, Walid doesn't consider me worthy of his friendship. But I love him, and I'm ready to help him at any moment. Would you kindly give that message to your friend?"

Diego, somewhat disconcerted, promised that he would. Again he looked around the room for Walid. And he no longer saw him or the other man. He was tempted to ask Michel more, but instinctively he let it go. Walid reappeared after a few minutes. He was back to his usual self.

"Shall we go have a drink?"

They ended up in a bar in Ponte Milvio, where they finished off two bottles of wine. Diego had never seen anyone drink with such conscientious concentration. They barely spoke, even though it seemed to him that, a couple of times, Walid was about to make some kind of confidence.

On the way back, he gave him Michel's message of friendship.

"He's a son of a bitch" was Walid's comment.

"In a good sense?"

"It depends, it depends."

They parted with a promise to meet again the first Saturday after the Christmas vacation.

Chapter 7

Diego, his wife, and the child spent a week with Elsa's family in a stormy, wind-whipped fishing village on the Adriatic coast.

It was very cold, and Giacomino came down with a severe flu. Sleepless nights and agitated vigils followed one another without a break: the child couldn't breathe, and, with his hysterical crying and his fixed, weary gaze, sought help and comfort that no one could give him. One night, the fever rose to 104 degrees, and he was shaken by convulsions. His crying faded to a faint, incessant wail in which Diego seemed to perceive the echo of a sorrow without hope, Elsa's tears became dry sobs, the grandparents shook their heads, sighing. It was he who resolved the situation by taking Giacomo in his arms and pressing him tight against his chest until his own breathing became one with the child's. He whispered an obsessive lullaby that after an hour got the better of the wailing, and until dawn he paced the rooms with the child in his arms, gazing into his uselessly staring eyes. Never as in such moments did he wish that a merciful death would carry off Giacomino, Yusuf, and all others like them. He wished for all unfortunate children and their desperate fathers a paradise of infinite blessings, where there was no distinguishing what is normality from what is not, where neither word nor movement nor sight nor hearing had any importance anymore.

Then, in the quiet of the morning, he regretted that desire, and thought of writing a letter to Walid. He thought of how he would begin, a sentence like "Who are we to judge" or "We don't have the right to judge," but soon he was overcome by a kind, restorative sleep. On waking, he realized that something in him was dying, to be reborn in a form whose novelty and difference he could grasp only in a confused way, and he missed his friend and that timeless time of their mute confidences.

The first Saturday in January he was told that Yusuf had been withdrawn from the institute.

"We don't know if he'll be back. His father spoke of a long journey."

Every attempt to find out Walid's identity was vain. Bound by confidentiality agreements, the workers responded to his requests with cold professional refusals. He asked the other parents for information, but all he managed to get was pious comments about the poor child with the narrow head, the son of that elegant Arab man whose name no one even knew. In any case, no one had ever heard talk of any Walid.

One afternoon he went to Mustafa's Turkish baths. The place was closed, the shutters lowered, with no sign of the old man with the turban and towel. Some shopkeepers told him that the Turk had been there before Christmas but since Christmas no one had been seen.

"Will he reopen?"

"If only I knew."

The following week the sky dumped a sensational snowfall on Rome and Giacomino was granted another excruciating bout of flu. Diego was the only parent who took his child to the institute that Saturday. Of Yusuf still not a trace.

Chapter 8

What followed was the saddest winter of Diego's life. Giacomo was racked by fevers that made him, if possible, even more absent, and as though exhausted by the work of existence. Elsa's obstinate refusal to resort to any form of outside help kept them from having the least social life. To entrust Giacomo to a babysitter, even if they could find one suitable for such a strange child, seemed to Elsa an inconceivable betrayal, like unloading him in some residential institute or delivering an aging parent to a hospice.

In principle Diego agreed, but the family was becoming a prison, and their solitude increasingly rancorous. He no longer went near his wife, and this had deepened the furrow that was pushing them apart, making them more and more intolerant. He had nothing to reproach her for, except the fact of her being there, beside him, sharing in vain so much suffering: deep inside, moreover, Diego felt an obscure sense of guilt for having drawn her into a venture that had no future.

Before Giacomo, his wife had had a job, a satisfying life. He had been the one to insist on a child, when the weight of solitary afternoons or a thousand routine tasks became unbearable to him, when he had begun to fear a barren future. Now Elsa reacted to his distance by withdrawing even further into herself, and Diego was convinced that she had given up not only hope but understanding. The negotiations for child-care benefits proceeded slowly, hindered by the administrative official in the local government health office, a bureaucrat with a red toupee who had let Diego understand in every way possible that in order to resolve the matter in his favor it would be necessary to "grease" the wheels of a certain machine.

There were moments when the wretchedness of his life seemed to him one of the many aspects, and not even the most unpleasant, of a more general misery: even as a normal person, Diego had never been able to think in terms that transcended the sphere of the everyday, but that winter he often felt that he was a sort of model of the general wretchedness, the victim of a conspiracy plotted by a bizarre demon to the detriment of humankind. We are here to suffer, he thought, and that creature laughs at us; it's as if our very suffering excited him. Ideas of persecution agitated his mind, he became aggressive, quarrelsome. At work, his colleagues avoided him, his boss reprimanded him for paltry matters; he got in the habit of allowing himself one glass too many.

One afternoon the family was honored by a visit from the parish priest, a young, sly-looking man who was preparing to bless the house in the name of the Lord. While his wife hurried to the kitchen to prepare coffee, Diego noticed that the priest was making the usual cajoling approach to Giacomo. Unable to control himself, he began spewing out at the priest everything he thought of his God. He expounded his theory of the bizarre demon, and, remembering his conversations with Walid, said that he preferred not to believe in the existence of such a spiteful entity. With growing indignation he added that, if he ever happened to meet him, he would try to strangle him with his own hands. The priest listened quietly, shaking his head. When, finally, he chirped a faint "I understand, my son, but you see . . ." Diego guessed that he was about to start singing the old song of resignation, and he grabbed the aspergillum from his hand and threatened to break it on his head. Elsa rushed in from the kitchen in alarm. The priest, hands joined, was praying. At the height of his fury, Diego noticed that the child, who had until then been crumpled in his orthopedic seat, seemed interested in the noise: he took part in his way, hurling little war cries, his cheeks red, his face open in a smile without guilt and without pity. Suddenly Diego was invaded by a sense of the complete uselessness of every form of rebellion.

He fled. He returned home at sunset. He found a full family council waiting for him, complete with a psychologist cousin who tried to persuade him to start psychotherapy, maybe in view of a second child. Disgusted, he ended up getting drunk in a seedy bar, where he was unceremoniously thrown out at closing time. Too drunk to remember where he had parked his car, he slept for four or five hours in a park near the Termini station, until, at dawn, he was thrown out of there, too. He didn't go to work that day, but within two weeks things had returned to normal.

A couple of times, Diego went as far as the Arabesque, but he didn't have the courage to face the club and the memory of Walid's party. Another time he happened to be in the neighborhood of the Turkish baths. The place had reopened, but he couldn't bring himself to go there, either. Out of cowardice and timidity.

One evening around the end of March, Giacomo had another convulsive fit. Diego tried to calm him, but this time his efforts were in vain. The tighter he held him, murmuring sweet little words, the more his head felt lacerated by the child's monotone sobs, a sequence of *eeh-eeh-eehs* that in the end got the better of his distraught nerves. Something broke inside him: he carried the child to the bed, grabbed him hard by the shoulders, and began to shake him with mounting fury. Giacomino didn't understand, couldn't understand. His eyes rolled, filled with desperation at that alien and now suddenly hostile world. Elsa tried to grab the child, shouting that he was killing him, but Diego violently pushed her away and continued until, with a last piercing wail, the child was nearly gasping for breath. Then, only then, he left him to his mother and locked himself in his study. It took him half an hour to master the trembling of his body. Hardly a sound came from the other room: only Elsa's voice singing a soft lullaby, and from time to time a slow sob from the child. Had he really thought of killing him? Would he have been capable of it? Had he known he was so violent? So cruel? But was it really cruelty? Yet he had to admit that he had been on the point of killing him. It had surfaced again, overwhelming him, that desire for death which would annihilate the idea of the future: for Giacomino, for Yusuf, for all children without a future. If he killed his child, he would spend the rest of his days in prison. But wasn't prison preferable to the sentence without appeal that defined his days? Yet this, too, he later confessed to a big glass of whiskey, was only an excuse, a pretext. He would never have had the courage to go all the way. He would never have done it. So he was also condemned to suffer for his weakness, day after day. He thought again of Walid. Now that Walid had vanished, he realized fully how indispensable that other suffering had become for him, a suffering so similar to his own that they could be identified as one unique, immense suffering. He cursed his friend because his departure had hurled him into a new solitude that, unlike the old one, would never be bearable. Because the old solitude had been interrupted for a brief moment by the warm breath of communion and the new was irremediable.

For ten days Diego and his wife slept in separate rooms, then everything went back to the way it had been. On Wednesday, May 14th, Zaira came to his office.

Chapter 9

S he was waiting in the corridor. Surrounded by door-keepers smelling of tobacco and security guards who were eating her up with their eyes.

She had been waiting for an hour because no one had deigned to tell him she was there.

"I have to talk to you."

With her hair gathered at the nape, a simple gold chain around her long neck, in jeans and T-shirt, and without a trace of makeup, Zaira seemed very different from the sophisticated Middle Eastern woman of the billiard game. A fresh, natural girl. But with a veil of anguish in her deep black eyes.

"Not here," Diego said.

They went out amid the tourists crowding Piazza Navona. Here she grabbed him by the arm and compelled him to look her in the eye.

"He is in danger. He needs you."

So, that was it. The great Walid needed the little Diego Marini. Diego smiled and lit a cigarette. Walid needed him! He felt a malicious joy that filled him with pride.

"Did you hear me? You have to help him!"

So he had become the hero of the story! But where the hell was Walid when I needed him? All he could say was, "Why me?"

"Why you? Because you're friends!"

At least, she had spared him that business of the two fathers! "Listen, you have your reasons. He disappeared suddenly, with no explanation, and goodness knows what you must have thought. But he couldn't do otherwise. He's in danger. I'm in danger, too. Oh, please help him! If they knew that I came to you, you, too . . . "

"They? They who?"

"They . . ." Zaira took it up hesitantly, "enemies . . . Walid can't go out during the day. They're after him . . . People capable of anything . . . "

They . . . enemies . . . danger . . . There were also children around . . . For a long time even the sight of other children had been hateful to him. Now it seemed to him that those children, all children, were beautiful. And when he came across one like Giacomo—by now it wasn't hard for him to recognize the signs—he thought, Look, one of us, a brother, isn't he beautiful, more beautiful than the others? . . . Enemies . . . he knew only one enemy, that pitiless and irrational God whom, with Walid, he had evoked one distant December morning . . .

"He'll be expecting you tonight at eleven at the old tufa quarry on the Ardeatine. It's not hard to find . . . Swear you'll go!"

Swear! He went off without even answering. The spiteful joy had vanished, the decision having been made as soon as Zaira said the first word. But it wasn't to her that he had to swear something: not to that woman. And not even to Walid. Only to himself did he owe something, even if it was just a stupid vow.

He reached the tufa quarry at ten-thirty, with a supply of cigarettes and of questions, and the secret desire for a warm embrace that would dissolve the nightmare in a fraternal sense of sharing. The quarry was a pit in the middle of a dirt hollow, a deserted area populated by rotting planks and the remains of old prostitutes' camps. There was a cold, high moon; from time to time clouds passed, of changing shape, now innocent sheep, now monsters with open jaws, and then the light returned to illuminate the desolate scene. Of Walid not a trace.

By midnight he had consumed the first pack. He heard a suspicious rustling, and, heart in his throat, approached a spectral bush, first whispering hopefully, then angrily shouting out the name of his friend. A cat leaped out from among the branches, eyes shining in the night.

Diego got back in the car after one and went to have a nightcap at a motel on the ring road. His solitary toast was dedicated to little Yusuf: may life be kind to you, wherever you are.

Chapter 10

The afternoon following Zaira's visit, Diego was approached by two men in blue suits as he left the Ministry.

"Doctor Marini? Follow us, please."

They stationed themselves at his sides, as if to prevent a possible attempt to flee.

"There must be some mistake . . . "

"No mistake," replied the one who had spoken to him, displaying a metal badge with an indecipherable inscription.

They walked him to a metallic-colored Fiat Croma that was blocking the entrance to the area reserved for official cars.

"Maybe a case of someone with the same name?" he said again, before getting in the car.

The two men exchanged a glance.

"Aren't you Doctor Diego Marini?"

"My name is Diego Marini, but I'm not a doctor."

"It's not a case of someone with the same name. Get in, please."

"Am I under arrest?"

"Just a formality."

They had him sit beside the driver, who was from the same mold as the other two, thickset men with smooth black hair, weak jaws, mirrored sunglasses, flakes of dandruff on their jackets.

Before he got in, he cast a last anguished glance around: what had he done? Why were they angry with him?

The car had an unmistakable odor, a mixture of old tobacco and cheap aftershave, worn leather and human sweat barely suppressed by the deodorizing tree. Once he had accompanied a high-level official to France for a deposition. They had traveled by car, a car with that odor. Odor of the state.

The three of them hadn't shown any I.D., but you could swear they were from the military police. He eyed the driver. He wore high black shoes, with squared tips and long, carelessly knotted laces. An old acquaintance of his, a sergeant in the Operations Division, had told him that criminals recognize undercover agents by their shoes.

"You can be a master of disguises, but what can you do, the shoes always give the cop away."

Those were, without the shadow of a doubt, cop shoes. Diego felt seized by an old panic. Why would the authorities have suddenly decided to take an interest in him?

The Croma turned onto Viale Trastevere, traveled to the end, and then took Via Oderisi da Gubbio, down beyond the bridge at the dog track, coming out on the overpass that led to Via Cristoforo Colombo. Finally, they left the city behind.

They turned toward the sea: the satellite city of Acilia or Ostia, if the Croma veered left at the interchange, or Anzio, Nettuno, and, farther on, Latina, if they went straight on the Via Pontina.

"Can you tell me what this is about?"

"We are not authorized to provide explanations, Doctor Marini."

He protested. It was a mistake, he couldn't imagine any justification for this sort of arrest. But he had the impression that they weren't even listening to him. The Croma took the exit for Acilia-Ostia.

Diego was in a cold sweat. He felt sharp pains in his stomach. He thought of Giacomino: soon he would be having his liquid dinner, just milk, because it was hard for him to swallow. He thought of Elsa, at this hour she would be wondering why he was late, maybe she would have called the office, but he had been the last to leave, and the office didn't have answering machines. He imagined those repeated rings, all the same, all vain, his wife's anguish, or maybe only her cold rage.

They had passed Acilia and Casalpalocco. Already the first houses of Ostia were visible.

Had he committed some crime, without realizing it? Could it be that Saturday when he had taken two hundred thousand lire from the office safe for an unexpected and urgent expense? He hadn't slept for two nights, and Monday morning, exactly at nine, he had made sure to replace the sum. He had vowed that such a thing would never be repeated, and years had passed, but maybe someone had found out, and now they were investigating . . . or maybe it had to do with the renewal of his license, or . . .

He retched, coughing to force it back down, while from his throat came a plaintive breathless gurgling. The driver smiled, a sneer that increased the tension. He wasn't brave, he never would be.

"We're almost there," one of the men in the back seat said, a hint of annoyance in his voice.

They went along the deserted waterfront drive at Ostia and then turned left onto a road lined with darkened villas. They stopped in front of a gate blocked by another metallic Croma.

"Here we are."

They escorted him through a garden that showed signs of neglect. On a bench beneath a three-bulb lamp someone had left a child's jacket. A cat was sleeping on it; at the sound of their footsteps on the gravel, it quickly vanished. The smell of salt and wet grass hovered in the air. A pleasant smell. Diego filled his lungs, and the sick feeling began to go away. The villa was completely empty; the walls bore the outlines of paintings that had once hung there. In a room whose floor was covered with dust and sawdust a man stood smoking a cigar. The light from a solitary ceiling lamp was too faint for Diego to distinguish his features.

"We've picked up the suspect, sir," said one of the two cops, coming to attention.

They were talking about him, he was the suspect! Diego instinctively retreated, his stomach clenched again in anguish.

The man advanced toward Diego. A tall man, heavy, with short gray hair and cold eyes of the same color.

"I'm sorry I can't even offer you a seat, Doctor Marini, but as you see the inhabitants of this house have taken care to deprive it of every comfort. Major Santini, of the Security Services."

Diego grasped the hand that the other extended as if it were his last hope, reassured by the cordial tone. Perhaps it was a mistake after all. It had to be a mistake. He wondered if that man would let him call home. Assuming that there was still a telephone in the villa. Just then he heard the roar of an engine, and realized that the kidnappers' Croma was leaving. So now it was just him and Major Santini.

"Would you like a cigar?"

"Thank you, I have my cigarettes," he answered, and brought a hand to his jacket pocket. Empty!

"They must have fallen out in the car . . . "

The Major gave an understanding smile.

"As the man said, in Italy no one can be denied a cigar or the title of *cavaliere*. Come on!"

He accepted. The sweetish aroma of the cigar disgusted him, but in order not to be impolite he held on to it. Sooner or later it would go out.

"And now, to us! So, Doctor Marini, you must have wondered what's behind all this. I would have preferred to warn you with a phone call, maybe we could have met in a less uncomfortable place, and I know that my subordinates are not monsters of sympathy, but you see, the fact is that some very recent events have forced us to accelerate things . . . Would you kindly glance at this photograph?"

He took it from the Major's hands and moved under the lamp to look at it. With his customary gentle smile, Walid stared at some indefinite point. So, it was about him. He should have realized that before. It didn't take great intelligence to make connections between the agents, the Croma, the villa, Major Santini, and the only event of any interest that had happened in his meager life. And, besides, what other motive could have impelled the Security Services to turn their attention to an insignificant government employee like him?

"So, what can you tell me about this photograph, Doctor Marini?"

"Let me look more closely . . . "

Yes, it really was Walid. His friend Walid. Zaira's words returned to his mind. Walid forced to hide, people looking for him. But why was all this happening?

"So?"

Who was Walid? A spy? A drug trafficker? A murderer? Why were the Security Services interested in him? Was he an enemy of his country? And how was he, Diego, to behave? The Major had taken him by surprise. His fault, his stupidity. He should have figured it out himself, immediately. He should have prepared some convincing response, he should have . . . But why, then, not tell the truth right away? What did he have to hide? A few brief encounters, shopping at the market, the Turkish baths, Zaira: what did he have to fear from the services? What did he owe Walid? He handed the photograph to the Major.

"What can I tell you? It's the first time I've seen him."

So, he had lied. And to think that he hadn't even realized it, as he uttered that apparently banal statement. He hadn't intended to lie; usually when he told a lie, he avoided the gaze of his questioner and his voice trembled. He had not intended to lie—it had been an automatic reaction. And his voice had sounded clear and he had withstood the Major's penetrating gaze. And how strange, that calm which had suddenly come over him!

"Doctor Marini, Doctor Marini! Don't make things more complicated."

"But really I . . . "

"Doctor Marini."

Now Santini's voice had become threatening. Diego felt a blind rage surfacing in him.

"I'm not 'doctor' and I don't know that man!"

"You are lying!"

Santini threw a pile of photographs at him. They had been taken in the area of San Lorenzo, near the institute. They showed him and Walid sitting at the table in the café, him and Walid in front of the pool hall, him and Walid with Giacomino and Yusuf.

The Major took his arm, cordial again.

"I understand, you know? In essence, our first contact was somewhat abrupt. I take all responsibility for it. But you must understand, this man you want to protect . . . to the Services he's known as Boutros Hosseini, but there is reason to believe that he has assumed at least half a dozen different identities . . . He is a clever, cultivated man, which makes him tricky and dangerous. Very dangerous, Doctor Marini. Now, we are looking for this man, and I think you can help us find him . . . You have no reason not to trust me, and above all you have no valid reason to protect this individual!"

No valid reason . . . Diego bent his head.

"But what has he done?"

Santini let a half smile escape.

"State secret! So? You recognize him?"

"Yes, I know him."

"Boutros Hosseini."

If that was the name known to the Major that would be the name known to him as well.

"Yes."

The Major nodded.

"It's obvious. This is, or, rather, was, his current cover. Doesn't matter. Tell me everything you know about him."

"Very little, in fact. We met by chance. He's foreign, has a nice car, a lot of money, I think everyone respects him . . . "

"What did you talk about, when you were together?"

"About our sons. They are ill."

"Oh, I'm sorry! Yes, yes, the institute . . . I understand, that's something tremendous . . . The children, the children . . . I feel for you, I feel for you, believe me . . . "

He put a hand on his shoulder, to emphasize that hasty sympathy. Diego moved slightly, murmuring an imperceptible thank you. The Major gave him another photograph.

It was Zaira.

"So?"

"I saw her a couple of times altogether. A friend of his."

"Melissa Kanakis?"

Again, if that was the name known to the Major . . .

"Yes."

"What sort of impression did she make?"

"A beautiful young woman."

Santini laughed, and shook his head.

"Good, good. You are cooperating. Excellent, Marini."

Diego drew a sigh of relief.

"May I go now?"

The Major seemed displeased.

"What do you mean! We've barely met and already you want to leave!"

"My wife will be worried."

"Just a moment's more patience."

"I've told you everything I know."

"Yes, yes, but listen . . . we need a small favor."

"From me?"

"From you, from you, Marini, precisely from you!"

"But I've never . . . "

"Leave the judgment to the professionals, dear sir. As far as we know, this Kanakis is just a marginal element. Probably she is involved in this unpleasant matter for sentimental reasons . . . You know how women are . . . But, anyway, we have a well-founded reason to believe that Boutros Hosseini has the greatest trust in her. And that she knows where our man is hidden. Now, for a complicated set of reasons that I cannot tell you, it's impossible to intervene directly with the woman. And this is where you enter into the game, dear Marini."

"Me?"

Santini took him by the arm and led him into the garden. The cat had returned, luminous eyes gleaming, to the child's jacket. Yusuf's jacket. The Major gave himself up to a convoluted monologue on the "logic of security," at the end of which he made Diego understand that what was urgent was not to lose the "contact."

"At present, you are our contact with Melissa Kanakis. And Melissa Kanakis is the only contact with Boutros Hosseini."

"Me? The contact? But if I don't even know what he does, where he lives . . . if you aren't able to find her . . . "

"True, true, Marini, but . . . that woman came to see you, at the Ministry, and not me . . . "

"You know that, too? Did you have me followed? So I am really a suspect?"

Santini shrugged his shoulders.

"I won't hide from you that some of my men find these associations of yours rather strange. Oh, but I reassured them, you know, because I have faith in you!"

He had put a hand on his shoulder, and was nodding, and looking into his eyes. Diego lowered his gaze.

"What do you want me to do?"

"Absolutely nothing. For now, wait. When you've been doing this job for a long time, and believe me, I'm one of the oldest in the business, you eventually acquire a certain sixth sense . . . I know that this Kanakis will come to see you again. And when that happens, you won't have to do anything but call this telephone number and tell me. Without delay. We'll take care of the rest. And you will have rendered a service to your country. And it will know how to reward you!"

Santini slipped a bill into his pocket and drove him back to Rome.

Chapter 11

Bewildering days followed. Small, insignificant events happened around him, and something decisive within. Zaira's visit had impressed his colleagues. He was credited with a fling with the unknown beauty. People who had always had contempt for him now sought his help. They talked to him about women, praised the beauty of Arabs. They asked him if "that young lady" had friends they could be introduced to. A department head confessed frankly that he would be willing to pay to spend a night with "someone like her."

Every protest he made was futile: curiosity increased and, with it, respect. Beyond that, the situation had its advantages.

His boss, for example. After harassing him for years, he suddenly began to show a keen sympathy for him. He didn't miss a chance to call him into his office on the most trivial excuses, shake his hand in an odd way, accompanying the gesture with a small pressure of his thumb on the inside of Diego's palm, and draw him into abstruse discussions on the need for men bound by certain strong ideals to join together to cooperate actively in achieving them. Diego wondered if Santini might be behind such an inexplicable change: but one of the aspiring lechers later confided to him that his boss had witnessed the scene with the men in the Croma and was convinced that Diego maintained who knew what sort of relations with who knew what centers of power. Besides, the man was a Mason, and must have taken Diego for a brother with whom he might undertake some lucrative business, advancing his career or creating a mini-mafia within the office. In the meantime, not only had he stopped tormenting him; he had relieved him of some irritating, burdensome tasks that had persecuted him for months. If nothing else, he gained precious time to think.

Santini was sure that Zaira would seek him out, and had told him to wait. And anyway, what else could he do? Yet he had lied to the Major. First unconsciously, as if a different and stronger will had replaced his, and then deliberately, because that reticence concerning the names of Walid and Zaira was nothing but a lie. But why had he done it? Did he want to start playing at spy vs. spy? Why?

It was an insistent and unbearable question: torture. Lying would have made sense if he had been Walid's accomplice. But he was no one's accomplice, he knew nothing of the other man, except that he was perhaps a friend, and surely a father as desperate as he. Was that the point? Friendship? Their shared condition? Had it been a form of confused loyalty that pushed him to behave like that? And to what purpose? And if Santini had guessed that he knew Walid's and Zaira's real names (assuming that Walid and Zaira were real names)? Even to someone as inexperienced as he it wasn't credible that an old fox like the Major would rely on a novice. Surely they were watching him; they had already done so. The Major was a professional; he would leave nothing to chance.

Diego got into the habit of looking around discreetly; at

times he found himself staring straight into the eyes of an embarrassed passerby merely because his physical features seemed vaguely Arab, or he telephoned friends he hadn't talked to for months, for the sole purpose of checking on whether there were suspicious noises, interference, or some strange click at the end of the conversation.

One evening, returning from work, he was sure he recognized, in the man positioned in a van a few steps from his door, one of the three soldiers who had escorted him to Major Santini.

That night he took out of a closet the old rifle his father had left him, and to his wife, bewildered by seeing him struggle with oil and cartridges, he said he had had a sudden desire to go hunting. But still the days passed, and Zaira seemed to have disappeared into thin air.

The only one who sought him out was Santini, with a phone call at the office.

"Still nothing?"

"Nothing new."

"You remember our agreement. And nothing rash."

Gradually, as time went on, he felt a pressing desire to disobey Santini growing inside him. And meanwhile the image of his friend recurred more and more frequently. He saw him wounded, hunted, hiding in some dank room, with his gentle smile and his sparkling eyes; he read on his lips an invocation, a cry for help, and imagined little Yusuf, his head drooping to one side, a thread of saliva on his lips, Yusuf half starved and abandoned, while evil men tried to take away his father, his only support . . .

A few days after Santini's phone call, he took Giacomino to the Roseto Comunale, the city rose garden, on the Aventine. It was a lovely afternoon, in a spring already resigned to the dominion of summer. Young couples and girls fresh from their first communion wandered among the sunlit arbors. He looked for a secluded corner, sat the child on his knees, and spoke to him, man to man.

"It was Walid who told me about the rose garden. I didn't even know it existed, imagine! Isn't it odd that foreigners know so much more about our city than we do? Now I don't remember if we were in the café or the pool hall. He was offended by an English poet who said that April is the cruelest month. Walid didn't agree. According to him the cruelest month is May, because it insults with its beauty. It was then that he said: 'I should take you to the rose garden. All that offensive beauty . . . We'll go together, to the rose garden, my friend. To be insulted by the beauty that our sons are denied.' I didn't know what to say: I never picked up a book of poetry in my life! Now that I'm here amid all these roses, I'm sorry he isn't here, too, because I would know what to say. I would say that I don't feel offended by their beauty. And I would also say to him that it's sad that you two children, you and Yusuf, can't enjoy it, the beauty of these roses, but that after all there must be some reason that justifies all this waste of petals and colors . . . What reason? I don't know, and maybe Walid doesn't, either, but it may be that the four of us together, you and I, he and Yusuf, if we join forces, might understand something . . . Only, now he and Yusuf aren't here, and the two of us, alone, what can we do? Don't you see how weak and defenseless we are? I need your advice. I think we have to make an attempt to find them. But I don't know where to begin. What do you think, Giacomino? If Santini gets him, we might as well give up. Those people are capable of anything . . . "

The child slid slowly to one side, his eyes made heavy by the drowsiness that inevitably came over him in crowded open spaces: his escape from the indecipherable world of others.

Diego went on talking to him quietly. He had something extremely important to communicate. Truths that he had come into possession of a few days earlier. Truths that burned inside him with the fury of revelation.

He told him that the following week he would be forty-three years old. Forty-three years of being told by others what was right and what was not.

"Don't you think it's time to say enough? The days go by and no one shows up. Maybe Walid managed to flee abroad, or maybe he's here, hidden somewhere, he needs us and we're not lifting a finger for him. And you know why? I'll tell you why, son. Because we're afraid. Sometimes I've even thought: it has nothing to do with me. I've done my part, and to hell with the rest . . . And yet it does have to do with us, it really does! You say: but what can we do, we don't know anyone, we don't even know where to begin. It's not our job. Let's leave it to the Santinis to take care of things. The professionals. Santini! I'd like to introduce him to you. You know what he said, Santini? That we have no valid reason to help Walid. No valid reason! What does Santini know about Walid! Did he ever see him blow on the face of his sick baby? No valid reason! And he says that to me! To little Yusuf's second father! After the questioning, Santini goes home to his family and his children, satisfied with himself, irreproachable, normal. I tell you who Santini is: a fake, a despicable fake. A thousand times fake and despicable! He says Walid is dangerous. But what Santini says isn't worth one of little Yusuf's toenails. It's not worth an ounce of your suffering, son. No, no, Giacomino, it's not enough to wait. Move, we have to move, and without wasting any more time!"

A family with children was walking by. A lively little boy stopped to look at Giacomino, then went up to him and took his hand. When Giacomo didn't respond to his entreaties, he said he must be a sleepyhead and went on his way laughing. The family disappeared over the horizon.

"I don't think we met by chance, Walid and I. No. It's something too important to be left to chance. You see, it's essential that I find him. We still have a long way to go together. Because ever since we met my life hasn't been the same. A lot of things have happened, all at once and all strange, and the strangest of all is that I know exactly what I'm supposed to do. Now, I mean. It's as if there were someone beside me prompting me with the right answer, the right move, the right question. Beside me . . . It's as if he were inside me . . . Tell me, isn't that maybe what that woman Zaira meant, when she said that now you and Yusuf have two fathers?"

Diego got up and put the child in the stroller.

"Say something, please!"

The child opened his eyes, stretched, then, recognizing his father's voice, stuck out his little hand to explore his limited horizon, and when he found himself touching his father's hairy hand, he broke into an angelic smile. Diego was filled with pride and grief.

"Good, son, the decision is made. And may Heaven protect us all."

Chapter 12

On his forty-third birthday, Diego brought Giacomo to the institute and, after loitering around the director's office for a while, waited until, at eleven, the secretary went off with a friend for coffee, and slipped quickly into the room, closing the door behind him. He figured that he had no more than ten minutes, and prayed fervently that no one would surprise him in that embarrassing situation. He had carried with him, in case he might have to force open some drawers or file cabinets, two screwdrivers and a rusty old hole punch. But there was no need: the files were in an open closet and, drawing on fifteen years of experience in government bureaucracy, he was able to find the "inactive" section right away. The diligent bureaucrat in charge had divided the files by year. Diego took the folder for the preceding year and began from the bottom. The last file was Yusuf's. He read the vital statistics: Yusuf Hosseini, father Boutros Hosseini, mother not stated, nationality Lebanese, born Paris 7/11/1991, resident in Rome, Via delle Sirene 25, tel. 06-949467. He quickly wrote everything down in a notebook, put file and folder back in order, and then, with a sudden second thought, tore out the picture of the child and put it in his pocket. He left the director's office and walked down a long corridor, at the end of which he ran into the secretary. He couldn't restrain a little smile of triumph: the ease of his venture had excited him. From the lobby of the institute he telephoned Boutros's house, but, as he expected, no one answered.

On Sunday he loaded the entire family into the car and drove them all to Ostia. He had pinpointed Via delle Sirene on the street map of Rome: if Santini's men were following him, an innocent family outing certainly wouldn't raise suspicions. He managed to happen casually onto Via delle Sirene, as though looking for a bath house that was not too run-down. And as they passed No. 25 he realized it was the uninhabited villa where his encounter with Santini had taken place. He wondered if the cat was still sleeping on Yusuf's jacket, and for the rest of the day was in a dark, irritable mood.

The next day he went back to work at the Ministry. Around noon he showed up at the security booth, exchanged a little chitchat with an old guard, and took him to the café for a coffee. According to regulations, all visitors not employed by the administration had to sign in at the entrance, leaving a photocopy of their identity card. The guards noted the day, hour, and purpose of the visit, as well as the name of the official visited. What he was looking for was the copy of the document that Zaira must have handed over when she came to see him. That was how he discovered that the person who had asked for him had registered under the name of Melissa Kanakis, Greek citizen. It was the very name that, according to Santini, Zaira had used. The document was a diplomatic passport issued by the Greek Embassy to the Holy See. From his office he telephoned the Embassy, and asked for Miss Kanakis.

Name unknown.

He persisted, trying to get any information he could, but was told that the Embassy issued on average two hundred and fifty passports a year, and that in any case any further information, regarding either the person requested or anyone else, had to be considered confidential. When the official asked Diego to give his name, he hung up abruptly. Then he looked in the telephone book, but he found no trace of Melissa Kanakis there, either.

So far, then, he had just been wasting time. The Major had told him that the girl had used false documents. And he had also said that Walid used cover names. He had wanted to check, not that he had had any illusions that he would track them down on the first try. In fact those first, uncertain moves on the path of the search had served to calm, but not, certainly, to satisfy, his craving for action. And then there was still the chance that Santini had lied: wasn't he, after all, paid to lie?

And if on the other hand it was Walid who had lied to him? If he really was Boutros Hosseini? How could Diego be certain that the Major didn't know his friend's real name? But why should Walid have lied to him? They were friends. Two fathers, friends . . . No, Walid had been sincere. It was he who was the repository of his friend's true identity. But now he had to do something different and more difficult.

At the end of his shift, he called his wife to tell her he would be staying late at the office to do some overtime. Then he stamped his timecard and tried the Turkish baths again.

What a change! The flaking walls had been replaced by a large room with rubber flooring and an aquarium filled with bright-colored fish. The place was teeming with instructors in warmup suits greeting overweight men and women in jeans with gym bags over their shoulders, and shunting them into areas marked by various signs: "Aerobics," "Machines," "Pool." A woman of around forty, dressed in black, with a string of pearls around her smooth neck, asked if she could help. Diego said that he was there for the Turkish bath. The woman asked to see his card. Diego replied that he didn't have one. But this was a private club, and to be admitted you had to pay a membership fee.

"Is there still a Turkish bath?"

"Of course, sir."

"I want to join."

After a series of formalities that seemed to him interminable, he signed at the bottom of a policy agreement and handed over half a million lire by way of deposit.

Then he had to get a bag, a bathrobe, and a bathing suit. Finally, he asked about a massage.

"I see that we haven't understood each other. This is a serious club," the woman replied, angrily. Diego realized his mistake, and explained that he was a former client of Mustafa's Turkish bath. The woman apologized, saying that the new management had taken over three months earlier, and that massages were not part of the "package." Then she handed him over to a young instructor, who led him down a long corridor with rooms opening off it, presided over by physical-fitness fanatics, and finally pointed out a locker and a small door. Diego undressed in silence, blushing under the gaze of a couple of regulars who seemed to judge his out-of-shape body severely, and went through the door.

The steam was so thick it took him some minutes to make out the bathers, who, stark naked, sat panting with their backs against the burning-hot walls, or tumbled, shivering, into the pool, to emerge refreshed.

He experienced again the oppressive heat of that far-off afternoon, and recalled his bewilderment. But how different it all was, how unrecognizable! Where was Mustafa, the silent masseur, the aroma of sweet coffee, the hookah and its heady flavor?

Meanwhile, dripping with sweat, he plunged into the pool, and had the sensation of suffocating. All his doubts came back, the fear of not being up to this, of making a mistake, of getting into some hopeless trouble . . . He was nothing but a mouse forced to follow a prescribed course leading to some unknown ultimate goal. Who could help him in this difficult moment, who would support him in this absolute void? No one, no one . . . He seemed to feel, for a moment, the evil gaze of the bizarre demon, and thought that perhaps the whole business was just an image dreamed up for the delight of that indefinable entity that took such pleasure in tormenting children and their fathers. Maybe at that precise instant it was observing him, enjoying his senseless agitation . . . He would have liked to cry for help, feeling again that he was suffocating, and decided that he would never be capable of doing any good. His thoughts turned to Giacomino. They had talked the other day, for the first time: his child had understood, he was sure, he felt it, but could he be sure that he had approved the decision? He had smiled at him, but . . . it was the smile of an idiot. Of the idiot son of that poor devil Diego Marini.

He would never make it; he would never be able to pull

it off. On the other hand, to abandon his friend to his fate—wasn't that like admitting yet another defeat? And it was no use telling himself that there had already been plenty of defeats in his life, and one more wouldn't change anything.

The water's icy caress gave him a useful shock. When he re-emerged, he heard talk all around him of a certain Anna, who must have been the lover of a lot of the men there. Vulgar adjectives were flying around, sent from mouth to mouth by those naked, sweaty men with doughy, acrid pleasure. But there was something unhealthy and morbid in their complicity: it was as if behind that display of virility the foreshadowing of the inevitable end could be sensed, along with a fierce desire to keep it away. Perhaps among those who had slept with that Anna ("a bit flabby but what a mouth," he heard one of them say, and coarse laughter emphasized the words) were some who had families, children. Healthy. Normal. And none were aware of the precious gift, the great good fortune that all of that represented. His complicity with Walid wasn't made of that. With his friend he had never talked about women, not in those terms, anyway. There was respect in what his friend thought, and respect in the way he said things. Respect for life. The respect of one who has known suffering and has been able to face it with strength. Walid had taught him many things. Why should he believe in the dark portrait that Santini had drawn? Walid was a father like him. Only a father. Always a father. For this reason he had to go on, even if the path seemed like a maze with no way out, even if the goal seemed unreachable. And Giacomino approved, he approved: it was for him, too, that he had to keep going. Yes, for him, too. And to hell with the bizarre demon: let him have his fun. He himself would have no peace until he had found his vanished friend.

At dinner, he realized that his wife was looking at him oddly. In order to avoid providing explanations, he kept his eyes fixed on the television. He offered to clear and clean up, loaded the dishwasher, helped Giacomo go to the bathroom (he couldn't do it by himself), put him to bed with a kind of dreamy delicacy that increased Elsa's astonishment, and spread around the bed the mosquito netting that protected the child from the bites of insects that he couldn't otherwise keep off. His wife waited for him, in her bathrobe, sitting in a chair, a cigarette between her lips. He couldn't remember ever having seen her smoke.

"We have to talk, Diego."

"I'm tired."

"There have been phone calls."

"What sort of phone calls?"

"Strange calls."

"What do you mean, strange?"

"Voices and music and then they hang up. What's happening?"

"Nothing. It must be some nut."

"Look, I don't like the way things are going."

"I'm tired, I'm sorry."

He went to bed, and stayed awake for a long time, aware of having gained only a precarious reprieve.

Chapter 13

The next morning there were six phone calls in less than an hour. Diego answered all of them. He heard some uproarious music, the sound of a juke-box with a strong echo effect, the rasping noise of someone breathing into the receiver, and then nothing. Before he left for work, he told his wife to take the phone off the hook.

When he got home at lunchtime, Elsa told him that there had been eight or nine more calls.

"I told you to take it off the hook. Tomorrow we'll change the number."

Throughout lunch, not a word.

Then, over coffee, the announcement.

"I want a divorce."

The telephone rang again. He answered. The show went on for a good half minute, then whoever it was hung up. Diego replaced the receiver slowly, and returned to the kitchen.

"I don't want to discuss it," she said curtly. But her eyes were swollen with crying. Giacomo was in a good mood, and with jerky movements of his head followed now one voice, now the other. Diego was overwhelmed by a wave of infinite pity. That was his life, his family. That woman who had once given him so much, the furniture in whose solid and reassuring shadow they had once been happy, or thought they were, that little world made up of orderly things that tried to resist the folly of existence . . . Was he ruining everything in pursuit of a meaningless adventure? Did he have the right to upset the lives of those who were close to him, who depended on him? Was he irresponsible?

"There is no other woman, if that's what you think . . ."

He tried to stay calm, even gentle. But would it be useful? Would it make sense to tell her about Walid and Zaira?

"That's not what I think, and anyway I told you, I'm not interested in discussing it."

It was he who had made her bitter, who caused her, with his apathy and his indifference, to grow distant. If he could just ask for a little time . . . He had to find his friend, help him, and then his task would be completed, and he would be able to return to his world, his life.

He lit a cigarette. His wife gave him a dirty look and pointed to the child, whose respiratory system was weak: since his birth Diego had been forbidden to smoke in the house. He put out the cigarette under a thin stream of tepid water. The washer of the tap was becoming capricious; in other times he would have taken care of the problem in half an hour—now it was likely to drag on for months.

"Maybe you should think about it a little, Elsa. You see, at the moment there are things going on that . . . "

Yet again he had mistaken tone, time, manner. Everything: he had got everything wrong, as usual. It was his hesitation that set his wife off. How long had she been keeping inside all those bitter resentments that only now she was finding the courage to express—and they were truths, terrible truths—and how much real pain was behind those furious eyes . . . As she told him what she thought of his disappearances, his neglect, his wretchedness as a man, she held the child tight, hugging him to her breast, making a shield of him, interrupting herself only to caress his head or plant desperate kisses, and he was overjoyed, and bending backward offered his neck to more kisses and more caresses. Finally the mother put him down and returned to the offensive, even more ruthlessly, her voice now reduced to a whisper.

The telephone rang again. Diego grabbed the receiver and shouted a curse into it, and then almost tore it off the wall. He took her head between his hands and whispered an entreaty.

"Just give me a little time. A month. Then I'll explain everything."

His sorrowful tone must have struck her. For an instant a trace of the affection that had bound them to each other flashed in her eyes. Even if there might not be time to put things right, Diego tried to insert himself into that unhoped-for breach. He spoke to her gently, lovingly, using words that came easily, lightly to his lips, and slowly he realized that the breach was widening, and that there was still a way to join their suffering, different yet similar.

Reluctantly, his wife agreed to a new delay: she would go to her parents for a month.

"I'll take Giacomo with me. Then we'll talk again."

While they were packing the bags, he was tempted to kiss her, to hold her in his arms, to make love with her the way they used to. He restrained himself out of respect for her suffering, out of decency, in order not to ruin everything.

He took them to the station. He got on the train with them. Husband and wife shook hands, and, giving the child a last hug, Diego got off the train and lingered on the platform, breathing in the odor of the ties and the track bed, long after the train had left the station. As a child he had desperately wanted one of those electric trains that, if you simply pushed the buttons on a bright-colored control box, came to mechanical life. He had often dreamed of plastic switches beside tin tracks, the locomotives with their smokestacks, the freight cars carrying Fiats destined for lucky, distant buyers. When he was asked, "What would you like to be when you grow up?" he answered, without fail, "An engineer." His parents didn't have money for a gift like that, and, besides, his father, for some unknown reason, considered trains a morally corrupting toy.

On the way home, he stopped in a big toy store and bought two electric trains, one for Giacomo and one for Yusuf. The designs on the big boxes showed trains with a futuristic look, very different from the ones that had been popular in his childhood.

Chapter 14

Later, he called Santini at the private number and told him about the phone calls.

"Good, good. That means we're on the right track. They're probably watching you. They still have to figure out how far they can trust you. But don't do anything. Keep waiting. Nothing rash, please. And keep me informed about everything."

He didn't like Santini's tone at all. As if the Major already knew about the telephone calls. Maybe his phone was tapped. Maybe Santini himself was behind the calls. Maybe he wanted to put pressure on him, to see how he managed . . .

He arrived at the Arabesque at nine that night. He knocked on the door and it was immediately opened by a gloomy-looking guard standing in front of an array of photographs of scantily clad dancers. Admission was free but you had to buy drinks. He went down the steep staircase and was surprised to find the place deserted except for a couple of bored-looking women who were talking to the bartender. No Arabs in fancy jackets, no jeweled ladies, the magic of the belly dance vanished. He wondered if, the first time he'd been there, it was his friend's presence that had lent glamour to a place that now appeared sordid and forsaken.

He sat down next to one of the women he'd seen talking to the bartender. A blond with improbably dark eyebrows, she was buried under a mask of makeup and perfumed by too much powder and too much deodorant. She wore net stockings and a short dress that allowed a glimpse of heavy breasts under the generously low neckline.

"Hi, my name is Gloria," she began, and, rubbing as if by chance against his thigh, asked him to buy her a drink.

"I'm Diego," he whispered. If it hadn't been for the darkness, she would have seen that he was blushing.

"Is this your first time at the Arabesque?"

"Actually no. But there's something that . . . "

"Listen," she resumed, practical, "you have to order something, if you don't I'll get the blame. Ask for a Coke, whatever, a lemonade. They'll give you a dirty look, but who gives a damn. The prices here—I can't even tell you. For a bottle of champagne, say, and not even the best, they're getting two hundred and fifty thousand lire. And if you dare to protest, there's a chance they'll beat you up. Anyway, if you're fond of champagne, there's always a nice bottle on ice at my place. I live nearby, and I'm much, much less expensive . . . "

The pressure against his thigh became more insistent. Gloria took his hand in hers, and began to caress it knowingly. Diego felt as if he were suffocating. The bartender was staring at him attentively.

"You decide," he said.

"Timid, eh?" the woman laughed. "Don't worry. I'll get you warmed up a bit, handsome!"

When she set off, hips swaying, toward the bar, Diego followed. There was no reason to stay sitting there like the designated turkey. All he had to do was take the few steps that separated him from the bar and ask for Michel. Hadn't the man sworn loyalty to Walid? Hadn't he asked him to bring Walid his message of friendship? He had barely moved when he felt a touch on his shoulder.

"My friend! What a nice surprise! What in the world brings you here?"

Michel had cut off his ponytail and was wearing an improbable lamé jacket open over his hairless chest. He led him to the bar, where Gloria had already had a bottle of champagne popped. The other woman, smoking a cigarette, looked increasingly bored.

"Come on, I want to introduce you to my friend Gloria."

"We've already met," she said, smiling, and added, pretending to be annoyed, "but you could have told me that you're a friend of Michel's. I would have spared you the farce."

"I didn't want to offend you," Diego answered.

"Imagine! With what walks through here every night."

Michel nodded, as if to get rid of the woman.

"Anyway," Gloria concluded, placing a kiss on Diego's cheek, "the offer is still good!"

The bartender called their attention to the open bottle.

"And who's going to pay for this?"

"On the house, amigo," and Michel, grabbing the champagne, led Diego off.

"Don't forget, the show begins at nine-forty-five," the bartender reminded him.

"Sure, with that big crowd waiting outside! Play some slow dances and forget about it, just listen to me!"

They sat down at another table, next to the piano. Michel poured the champagne.

"To Gloria's health. A really fine woman, right? Plus she knows how to do certain things . . . Oh Lord, you didn't come here without condoms? If you want, I always have a supply . . . "

"That's not what interests me, Michel."

The other stared at him skeptically.

"Surely you don't . . . I mean, if you like men, you shouldn't be ashamed, you know. I have a lot of friends who . . . "

How was it possible that Walid had had any sort of intimacy with that pimp? Diego stared hard.

"Look, it's serious. It has to do with Walid."

Michel smiled. But there was a light in his eyes that Diego didn't like at all.

"Our friend hasn't been seen for a while," he said knowingly.

Diego remembered Walid's warning: a son of a bitch. But he had also added, when questioned, "It depends, it depends." Well, he would behave accordingly.

"He sends his greetings."

"Really? I am honored. What can I do for you, my friend?"

"I'm looking for a girl."

"Good, then you're in the right place."

So did he not want to understand? Or was he pretending not to?

"Not any girl. A friend."

He described Zaira, in a roundabout way. Michel sat watching him for a while, with that far from reassuring look, and then pointed a finger at him.

"Tell me, you wouldn't be looking to steal Melissa, eh?"

Melissa, always Melissa! Diego felt disoriented. He

blushed. He caught, from the Armenian-Greek, the same air of obscene complicity he'd seen among the men at the Turkish baths.

"It's just a business matter," he said, but his trembling voice betrayed his indecision.

"I understand, I understand."

The other had nodded, and then allowed himself a meditative pause. There was that flash again. A flash of greed.

"You're asking a lot, my friend," he said, finally.

"It's important. Very important."

"I understand. It's difficult. But it's also true that nothing's impossible, when it comes to real friendship!"

"Tell me where she is."

"My friend, I don't know. But even if I did, before I told you I'd have to know if she agrees. Don't you think?"

The bartender came over and said something to Michel in Arabic. Michel got up and, telling Diego to wait for him, headed toward the piano. He greeted the audience—two very tall blacks in U.S. Navy uniforms who were negotiating with Gloria and the other girl—and started on "Summertime."

To Diego it seemed that Gloria smiled at him. But maybe it was only an illusion.

Following "Summertime" came "The Man I Love" and a ragtime tune to which Michel added some improvised vocalisms. His voice wasn't unpleasant, but, despite all his efforts, the atmosphere wasn't even close to warming up, and the place still had an odor of melancholy. Three middle-aged Japanese men arrived, and two more girls like Gloria emerged from some secret door. The musical repertory changed, from thirties jazz to Neapolitan song. The sailors seemed not to like it, while the Japanese, excited, clapped in time. Gloria, hand in hand with one of the sailors, passed by his table, and this time he was sure she winked at him.

Michel stopped playing after a beguiling "Reginella." The place was filling up: now it was the turn of a group of men in their fifties, muscular types who looked like farmhands. Three more girls emerged from the same door. Where had they been hiding all that time?

"Did you see all these people? Come and visit us more often. We haven't had a crowd like this since the night of that famous party . . . "

"Melissa," whispered Diego.

Michel snorted.

"Yes, of course, Melissa. Very high-price stuff, my friend."

Another rapacious look.

"She hasn't been seen around here much lately, either. She's changed her circle. New friends, another milieu. However, however . . . let me think a little . . . one could try asking . . . but it might cost a little money."

"How much?"

"Let's say a million, all-inclusive, eh? It's a matter of finding the right path. And in this, let it be said, Michel is a real master!"

Diego tore off the check without even trying to bargain. He was just in a hurry to get out of there.

"So we understand each other," the other concluded, grabbing the check. "Give me three days and I'll set up a meeting with your girl."

"Three days is too many. Tomorrow."

"You're joking? Make it two days."

"All right, two."

"Listen, give me your number."

"Why?"

"When I've got a deal, I'll call you. Better that you not call me. I wouldn't want them to think here that . . . "

"What are they supposed to think?"

"Nothing, nothing, trust me! And say hello to our friend, when you see him."

Why had he emphasized that last phrase? Diego wrote his number on a piece of paper and Michel returned to the piano. The ruddy farmhands asked for "La Bella Gigogin" and "Quel mazzolin di fiori." Gloria's friend and one of the black sailors had disappeared, other girls were moving in the shadows with the Japanese. Diego finished his champagne, warm by now, and left, saying goodbye to the bartender, who responded with a wave of a cocktail shaker.

He had just got outside when Gloria joined him.

"You're ending the evening all alone?"

"Maybe another time, I'm tired tonight."

"Pity. But come see me, eh?" the woman said, and kissed him on the mouth.

Later, as he was trying to sleep, he wondered if Walid would approve of his conduct. He wasn't so worried about trusting a shifty man like Michel: at this point, any clue, even the slightest, might be decisive. A different thought preoccupied him: that girl, Gloria. Her kiss had aroused him. He had always been faithful to his wife, but now Elsa was far away, and unusual things were happening to him . . . He wondered what would have happened if the woman had insisted. He wondered how it might be to make love with someone so different from his Elsa. And while he wondered, he seemed to feel, in some way, corrupt, dirty. In an old book, as a boy, he had read that the ancient knights were supposed to remain chaste for the duration of their mission. But the book didn't specify if the knights had the right to get excited. He, in spite of everything, felt excited. This would have been impossible to explain to Elsa. But Walid, he was sure, would have understood. At midnight he called his in-laws. Elsa and the child were asleep.

Chapter 15

The next day, leaving the Ministry, he was enveloped by a strange languor, and decided to take advantage of what was perhaps a unique opportunity. All that free time at once . . . He sat outside at a café, in the center of a piazza in Trastevere. The tables were crowded, with tourists and neighborhood people, people who could afford to sit in the sun and have an aperitif without the pressure of having to get back to work. He ordered a sandwich and a beer. It was years since he had gone out to lunch, and the taste of the fake homemade food seemed thrilling. He thought again of Michel, of Gloria. The excitement of the previous night had not vanished, in fact. And he continued to feel in part elated, in part dirty and corrupt.

A couple moved among the tables: the man was ragged and gave off a bad odor, the woman had long, straw-like blond hair, unwashed, and was carrying a dirty child with enormous, catlike eyes. They were begging, holding up a refugees' ID card, or something like that. Two well-fed men in their fifties, sitting in front of him, momentarily interrupted their reading of left-wing newspapers to rudely chase away the intruders.

In the meantime, the little family had approached his table. The child, although obviously undernourished, seemed lively, to judge from the way her eyes darted this way and that. When the man held out his hand, Diego, without much thought, took out his wallet and handed him a bill. The man smiled, with an embarrassed half bow. The child clapped her hands happily. Maybe it was a way her parents had taught her of saying thank you.

"There are still people who fall for that," commented a woman sitting to his right. Her mirrored sunglasses reflected the rainbow of a tropical cocktail.

"They're drug addicts," the woman sitting with her explained. "Did you see how they keep that child? A disgrace!"

Diego felt inexplicably wounded. To him she had seemed a beautiful child. A beautiful happy child.

"She should be taken away from them, certainly!" said the first woman.

"Given to respectable people," the second confirmed.

"Anyway, she's a lovely child," Diego said, aloud. He gulped his beer, paid, and quickly left.

The excitement had vanished; now there was only a feeling of something sordid and a painful confusion.

All day his anxiety grew, and finally he went into a movie theater, without noticing the title of the film. It was a Western: he had once been a fan of cowboys and Indians. But he soon realized, with great disappointment, that things had changed in recent years: the good guys were bad men who, by pure chance, found themselves fighting on the right side, and the bad guys were noticeably more sympathetic; and then, over all, there was a cynical tone that left him dismayed. At the end of the film, he went home and took refuge in his bed with a sense of relief.

The next day he didn't feel like facing the office. The air over the city had grown sultry and oppressive. He made coffee and took it out to the balcony. As he walked through his apartment, its three rooms, kitchen, and bath, he seemed to hear the echo, from somewhere, of Giacomino's labored breathing. He wasn't used to being alone in the house. The street exhaled an anguished symphony of noise. There were sudden bursts of shouting against the constant background noise of traffic. In the distance, flocks of starlings whirled through the sky beyond the darkened line of the horizon, veiled by threatening clouds. Maybe it would rain tomorrow.

It had also rained on that Saturday morning. By mutual agreement, he and Walid had decided to skip the therapy and take the children to the zoo. A bad idea. The broad pathways were deserted. The tropical birds and the big mammals uttered their hoarse cries, a few drowsy zookeepers placed bits of bloody meat in the cages, the monkeys flitted from tree to tree as if crazed. The children huddled in their strollers, too frightened to sleep, too withdrawn to participate. Both Yusuf and Giacomo had suffered, from unknown causes, irreparable damage to their sight. The only functioning channel of perception was hearing. Sound was their window onto the world, but the world had too many sounds, too diverse, for their small, malformed brains to take in.

Walid had stopped before a cage isolated from the others. There was a monkey inside, with pure blue eyes and fair skin devastated, here and there, by spots of an ugly grayish color. The animal was indifferent to their approach; it was clear that it was depressed, and not in the mood to show off for the human population. A guard warned them not to get close, because the beast was sick and in isolation, and could be contagious. The fathers looked at their sons, then Walid asked if that sick "hamadryas" was for sale. The guard said that the animal would soon be dead, and in any case private citizens were forbidden by law to keep exotic pets.

They resumed their walk, maintaining for a few minutes the most absolute silence. Then Walid said that when it had all ended he would like their children to live together.

"All what?" Diego asked.

"There is always something that has to end."

The other's answer had disoriented him: as usual, he hadn't understood and had given up trying. Now that he had more elements on which to base a judgment, now that he could see more clearly within himself as well, he felt that he was able to give the right interpretation to his friend's words. It was as if Walid had been trying to tell him that he had to get out of some dangerous situation, and that he had to do so for Yusuf. For that same reason, he, Diego, had to help him. And, further, he felt that he owed Walid something precious, which he could never give up. It was something more profound and noble than the foolish sense of excitement that had beguiled him for a few brief moments. He still didn't know clearly what it was, but he felt indebted to him.

Then, around nine in the evening, when it seemed that he could no longer contain his anguish, Gloria telephoned.

"Michel wants to know if you can come over here, to the Arabesque."

Chapter 16

It was off hours, as it had been two nights earlier, and the club and its women were showing their true face of desolation and neglect. Gloria was talking to the bartender, but as soon as she saw Diego she abandoned him and took Diego by the arm.

"There's been a change of plan. We're going to my place and he'll join us."

"But don't you have to work?"

She said she was tired of being fondled by drunks and old Japanese men.

"And besides, for friends this and more!"

He followed her obediently. Gloria's apartment was a real surprise. Small, neat, with no trace of her disorderly life. On a chest was a photograph of a smiling child.

"Is that your daughter?"

"It's me as a child. I wasn't always like this, you know."

There was a small sofa with hand-embroidered antimacassars. Diego sat down with a sigh and took the whiskey she offered.

Gloria sat beside him. She continued to study him with her small eyes, now sly, now vaguely absent. He asked her about Michel.

"Oh, he'll come, he'll come, you can be sure. You paid

him, no? When that man gets the scent of money he'll go to the ends of the earth."

For the moment, then, he was alone with Gloria. With the woman who had aroused him two nights earlier. Her plunging neckline gave a generous view of her heavy breasts. Her fishnet stockings designed tiny rectangles of pale skin under a short skirt. And yet there was something strange, different about her, an excessive animation, an exaggerated nonchalance. As if she had been assigned the task of putting him at his ease.

"What did Michel tell you?"

"Nothing. All I know is I'm supposed to keep you here quietly until he deigns to show up."

Her perfume was more delicate, less aggressive than he remembered. Now that they were so close, now that their bodies were touching, Diego again found her desirable. It would be easy to have her, basically she was . . .

"Did he tell you what time he was coming?"

"Hey, what's the hurry! And then, excuse me, I might be insulted. Here we are, the two of us alone . . . And all you do is ask me about Michel, Michel this and Michel that . . . You two aren't not engaged, are you?"

She put one arm around his shoulders and tried to draw him toward her. That's how she was: like that Anna they were talking about at the Turkish baths. Available, with a good mouth. Desire became a subtle form of unease. He sat upright on the sofa, pushing her back.

"O.K., whatever you want. I was just trying to make the time pass. But you're a strange guy, you know? Tell me what business a guy like you has with Michel? You seem normal, it's obvious from a mile away that you have nothing to do with these people. When I came on to you the other night, I said to myself, Gloria, if you can't get a hundred from a guy like that, well, it's time to retire . . . And instead here you go and hand the pianist a bribe and then you don't even want to make love . . . Either you're strange or you must have some big problem."

"I have a problem."

"And Michel is helping you solve it."

"Yes."

"Then I understand," Gloria concluded. "Wait a second. I have what you need."

She disappeared for a few moments, and reappeared with a red tin. She opened it and took out a grainy powder of small pink crystals, which she arranged in small lines on the table in front of the sofa. She rolled up a ten-thousand-lire banknote, stuck one end in her nostril, aimed the other at one end of the line, and inhaled vigorously. The small pink crystals disappeared into the funnel of the bill.

"Go on, you have a line," she said to him, in a slurred voice, handing him the bill.

"Is it drugs?"

Gloria looked at him in astonishment.

"You really are an oddball! This is Bolivian pink. Hundred percent pure. Strong stuff. First you get high, then you screw."

Diego shook his head.

"O.K., do what you like. If you're happy . . . "

The woman inhaled again, three, four times, and when all the crystals had disappeared, she licked the banknote. Diego looked around. He had to get out of there. Gloria had fallen back on the sofa, her eyes closed.

Diego sat there gazing at her, caught between attraction and repulsion. How could he have come to this? And

Gloria, had she really once been the girl in the photograph? I wasn't always like this, she had said. But what roads must one take to become so different? Were they the same as Walid's? He couldn't believe it. It wasn't possible.

"I can't stand drug addicts," Gloria was saying, her voice made hoarse as if by an immovable lump in her throat, "imagine, today they arrested two addicts who shot up their seven-year-old daughter with heroin. There's so much misery around! Yesterday a Peruvian woman abandoned her infant, a few days old, on the steps of a church, because she was too poor to keep it. So much despair! A week ago the father of a handicapped child went mad, strangled the child, and then turned himself in to the cops."

Why that mention of the handicapped boy? Maybe Gloria knew? Who was this woman really? Diego had a sense of danger.

"Are you trying to tell me something?"

"I'm not saying anything. I don't know anything. If you do a little of this, we'll make love and it will be beautiful."

The telephone rang. Gloria reached out a hand for the receiver. She exchanged a few words and the apparatus fell out of her hand. Diego picked it up. The person had hung up.

"Wow!" Gloria jumped up, all red and sweaty. "The downer is over. You really are a shit. To have stuff like this within reach and pretend it's nothing. You really are a shit. By the way. That was Michel. He's waiting for you outside. And when you see him, tell him not to send me another shit like you."

He went out, followed by her laughter. On the street he looked around for the Armenian. Except for a big black car, the street was deserted, an island of small buildings between two strips of open countryside. The moon was veiled by clouds. Shadows emerged from the black car. He didn't realize that they were coming toward him until they were on him. Two brawny young men, trained for that kind of work. Without giving him time for the semblance of a reaction, they went for him, kicking and punching. He tried to protect his face, shielding it with his arms, but he ended up on the ground. They kept on beating him. In utter silence, like robots, not even breathing hard with the effort. Tireless robots. An explosion of voices. A man and woman were quarreling in an unknown language. The beating stopped: his fate seemed to depend on the outcome of the quarrel. The woman had an imploring tone, the man spat out brusque, guttural phrases. Diego, on his back between a puddle with an acrid smell and a urine-soaked cardboard box, was barely able to look up: he could make out only murky shadows. More kicks. The woman shouted, the man growled something like an ultimatum. More blows, less confident this time. He closed his eyes. He heard the men going off, and the car doors close, and the rumble of the engine starting; he opened his eyes and was caught for an instant in the glare of the headlights, then he heard heels beating on the pavement, and was wrapped in a cloud of perfume. For a moment he thought the face leaning over him, framed by black hair, must belong to Gloria. He thought there might still be a spark of humanity in her, but then he remembered that Gloria was blond, and he lost consciousness.

Chapter 17

He dreamed he was running away: someone was chasing him, a vague entity, threatening. A woman was with him: she had his wife's voice and Zaira's clothes, but no face. Together with her, he sought refuge in a hospital. A child was asleep on a gurney placed under a large tube that made a sinister buzzing sound. A doctor showed him some X-rays on which the contours of the child's skull appeared. In a metallic voice, he explained to him that the scattered white areas indicated the developed parts of the brain, and the many, too many, black holes were the sacks that would never be filled with gray matter. Then they took the child away from the tube and handed him over. It was Yusuf. The woman laughed. They were on a street: he gave the child to the woman and walked north. Walid was there waiting, against the sky. With him was Giacomino: the child was waving to him with his little hands. He went toward them, but with every step the distance increased. He realized that he would never reach them. The earth began to revolve all around him, as if he were in the middle of an earthquake, rough hands seized him, and with a cough he woke up.

"Your papers," said a harsh voice.

He had just managed, with a great effort, to open his eyes, when a violent light forced him to close them again.

"Papers," the voice repeated, and the shaking began again.

It took him a while to realize that he was in a car, his car. But how had he gotten there? Three policemen in uniform were going through the usual procedures. As they continued to torture him with the light, and he regained a vaguely upright position, he remembered Gloria and her cocaine, and the men who had beat him, and the figure leaning over him . . .

As he came out into the open, he noticed that dawn was rising, a milky dawn that promised the torrid heat of the usual haze of toxic gases. He had a pain in one side and his clothes were in tatters. He searched his pockets mechanically. They had left him his wallet. He handed his license and identity card to the head of the patrol.

"So who did the number on you?"

Diego shrugged. The head of the patrol ordered him to open the trunk. The man searched in the space where the spare tire was kept, fingered the rubber duck that had been Giacomo's first toy, then closed the trunk. "Are you drunk?"

Diego shook his head no. The cop seemed to look at him with a minimum of pity, while his companions radioed headquarters with the information on the license. They were young, faces puffy with sleep and with resentment toward that poor jerk who had thought it a good idea to sleep off a drunk in the middle of the street . . . Yes, but what street? He saw tall buildings, an overpass in the background: they had taken the trouble to move him, but where had they brought him? The radio crackled something. The cops looked at him, then exchanged a glance and a couple of remarks that he couldn't catch, and finally the chief gave him back his documents.

"Go home, you're better off."

He thanked them with a nod, got behind the wheel, and realized he had no keys. The squad car took off, tires screeching.

He couldn't find his keys. He got out of the car. He looked up and saw the neon sign of an investment company. At that hour of the morning it was still off, but soon, very soon, it would began to deliver its luminous flashing message, promising needy families "quick, easy money at ridiculous rates." He had been looking at it for twelve years, that sign. Ever since he had come to live in that anonymous suburb. Why had they left him a hundred meters from his house? Maybe to prove to him that they knew everything and could do anything? He went on foot. The door was half open. And yet he had closed it when he went out, the evening before, didn't he always remember to do that?

The apartment presented a scene of devastation: all the furniture had been moved, the drawers emptied, papers were everywhere, the mattresses had been ripped open. Not even the two electric trains had been spared, and the futuristic locomotives lay overturned, sadly, beside the tracks, whose microscopic ties had been torn out one by one.

In the kitchen was Major Santini. In shirtsleeves, with a *cornetto* and a cappuccino.

"Go get cleaned up, Marini, you need it. I'll wait, I'm not in a hurry."

His voice was icy, his tone reproachful.

A quarter of an hour later he joined him in the living room. Undressing, he had found, in an inside jacket pocket, the car keys. In the shower he made an effort not to think.

He would have liked to have his child with him. Talk to him.

The Major had righted two chairs, and arranged them facing each other, and, sitting with his legs crossed, was smoking a pipe with a dry, pungent aroma.

Diego remained standing, leaning against the window.

"You know what you've done, Marini? You've ruined everything."

"And so you took it out on my son's toys?"

"Details. What counts is that you've caused my mission to fail."

Diego would have liked to tell him that he didn't give a fig for his mission. But he felt tired, drained. He confined himself to lighting a cigarette.

"Marini, Marini! What were you trying to prove?"

"Me? Nothing. It seems to me that we're on the same side."

"You went looking for them in their lair, you asked imprudent questions, you put them on the alert . . . And do you know who will pay for this? Your friend Walid! That's what you call him, right?"

"Yes," Diego confirmed, dully, "that's the name of Yusuf's father."

"We could have saved ourselves a lot of trouble if you had been more trusting. I ask you again: what were you trying to prove? That you're smarter than us? Answer me, say something, for God's sake!"

"You didn't trust me . . . "

"On the contrary. It's precisely because I trusted you that we're in this mess. I should have thrown you in jail, Marini, made you feel the iron fist. And instead . . . and instead we've wasted oceans of time . . . And all because I didn't want to force the situation . . . The honest and loyal Diego Marini! Bound by an incomprehensible sympathy to a bunch of crooks. And it was all my fault! Let's give him free rein, that boy. He'll understand and he'll behave. I've been stupid, stupid! But let me tell you: the fault of anything that might happen . . . that might already have happened . . . the fault is yours!"

Diego thought of Giacomo, he thought of Yusuf, he thought of his far-off friend. He thought of his own wretchedness and his failure, and felt like crying. Santini pressed him.

"What you didn't want to understand, because you were not up to understanding, is that we also want to save your friend Walid."

But why? Hadn't he told him that Walid was a dangerous criminal? Why did there never exist a single truth, why did everything seem to be drowning in a magma of betrayal and confusion? Santini had jumped to his feet, and was pacing up and down the room.

"Why do you think he's hiding, eh? Why is he afraid of us? No sir, no sir. Damn it, Marini, Walid broke with his clan. That's why he's hiding, because he's afraid of his old friends. Walid is a professional, he knows the rules of the game perfectly. He knows the risks and the benefits. There are procedures that only professionals can understand. We and Walid are now on the same side. And if the other side gets its hands on him, it's over for him. What we find of his body will be no bigger than an ear."

And to emphasize the weight of his assertion the Major made a meaningful gesture with the thumb and index finger of his left hand.

"That sympathetic Turkish gentleman who responds to

the name of Mustafa Necpez, for example . . . you remember him, right, the owner of the Turkish bath?"

Diego nodded.

"Good. Nice person, generous, a real friend, don't you think? You should know that in his country he was sentenced to death two or three times, in absentia, for a series of crimes that would give you gooseflesh just to hear them enumerated . . . They call him *hanca kara dayi*—the black uncle. Cutting off ears is one of his methods, and not even the bloodiest. Which shows you the kind of people your friend Walid used to hang around with until more recent events . . . Damn it, you should have just stayed waiting quietly until that girl showed up. We would have taken care of the rest. And instead you've ruined everything, everything! You went to see Michel Agambanian. That stinking son of a bitch who . . . "

"He said that, too."

"Who?"

"Walid. He said that Michel is a son of a bitch."

"You see? You see? Because he's a professional, he knows how to judge men. You were lucky to get away with a few kicks. You can see they're still hoping to fix things up . . . But me, no, I have no more hope!"

Diego took his head in his hands. Walid knew how to judge men, and had trusted him. But Walid had been wrong. He was just a good-for-nothing. They had all trusted a good-for-nothing.

"Bravo, now you're in despair, now that it's too late. For me, the game is over. As for you, I still have to make a decision. For the moment, consider yourself temporarily free. It may be that you are just stupid, but it may also be that there's something else there."

When the Major left, Diego telephoned Elsa's parents. His wife answered.

"I want to speak to Giacomo."

"He's sleeping."

"Now!"

He waited a few minutes. Then he heard the wailing of the little boy, disturbed in his difficult sleep.

"I failed," he said, and hung up.

Chapter 18

Putting the house back in order, he came across a small black leather bag containing dusty papers and old photographs. Among them was a kind of pastel-blue report card that showed little bears around a dripping honeycomb and the words "For my child" beneath a discreet ad for a line of food products. It was a brand that meant nothing to him, an old company of which by now even the memory was lost. He opened the report card, and recognized his father's tidy handwriting: it was his "baby record," in which, scrupulously noted, were the progressive weights, heights, and evolutionary advances of the first three months of life of Diego Marini.

"At thirty days he has six meals for the equivalent of 180 grams of powdered milk"; "On the forty-fifth day he skips his night feeding and sleeps for seven hours, until seven the next morning"; "At sixty days he holds his head up, supporting himself on his arms and orienting his gaze to right and left"; "At the end of his third month drooling and biting his fingers on the left side of his mouth. Is he getting his first little tooth? Precocious?"

He was surprised to find himself making comparisons with Giacomino: for four months Giacomo had refused any form of nourishment, he was lovingly force-fed for hours and hours, for the sole purpose of keeping down a few grams of milk between bouts of vomiting. He had held his head erect for a few seconds after the first year of life; he had never slept for an entire night, all the lullabies and sedatives of this world were useless for a brain that received continuous charges of electricity from inside . . . At the institute the parents had been warned to avoid comparisons between their child and other children. It is, the doctors had explained, a pointless and damaging exercise: the criteria of commonly accepted normality for an ordinary child couldn't be applied to children like theirs. These continuous comparisons are what cause many people to reject handicapped children. Crossing the frontier of normality had been their imperative—his and Elsa's—and there had been moments when he felt he was going mad, because they had plenty to say, and suggest, the doctors, the experts, the strangers, but his son had been denied the right to live, and at the same time would live: a life on the threshold of permanent darkness.

Now that by pure chance he had found himself comparing Giacomino with himself as a child, he felt a different uneasiness, a kind of subtle and bitter sadness, no more stinging than recent wounds, but sustained uniquely by the memory of a past injury. He looked at himself again in the old photographs: nursing in his mother's arms, chubby, selfish, tyrannical like all newborns, victims of those loving gazes, those warm embraces that they will forever after long for; at three, sitting in precarious equilibrium in the center of a vast armchair, dazzled by the flash; at six, in a red jacket with yellow buttons, a huge gap between his front teeth, bewildered by the presence of a big cake with six candles; at eight, fearfully thin, and with very short hair, embracing a dog with an enormous tongue hanging out, a mutt that had ended up under a truck one summer morning . . .

All these reassuring banalities, which represented the regret and pleasure of memory, were denied to his son: Diego wondered if, embarking on this risky adventure, he had, in some way, intended to make a gift to Giacomino of an undertaking that in his eyes would appear exceptional. A gift, and also compensation for all that the world would never give him. But does it make sense to give something to someone who can't understand? Is it not perhaps a sin of pride disguised as altruism?

Another thing they had told him at the institute: children like Giacomo have a morbid sensitivity to everything that regards their own affective sphere. These creatures "feel" love, distrust, hatred, and rejection. Ever since he had dedicated himself to Walid's cause, Diego had begun to talk to Giacomo and, since then, the child had "felt" him in a different way. He loved him more, in other words: he was sure of that. And so there was a gift and there was a compensation. And there had been, in his intentions, something that the twisted logic of a Santini couldn't even conceive. Now of all this nothing remained. Only a sensation of utter emptiness. He burned the report card and the photographs, and threw the black leather bag in the trash can. In the future, comparisons would not be possible.

In the hottest part of the day he was overcome by drowsiness. The sound of the telephone woke him. It was evening, the house was illuminated by the dying light of sunset. Diego answered automatically. Elsa's voice was icy.

"A woman called."

"What woman?"

"She didn't give her name. She sounded foreign."

"She was looking for me?"

"She told me to tell you that Dr. Hosseini will expect you at ten at No. 1300 Via Appia Nuova."

"Elsa . . . "

"What is it?"

"Tell Giacomo that the game is on again."

Outside it was raining.

Chapter 19

The appointment was in front of an abandoned factory. A crooked sign announced that, inside that large shed with broken windows, ball bearings had once been produced. Occasional vehicles sped by on the Appia Nuova, leaving Rome. Not far away, a transvestite with a long blond ponytail was negotiating with two teenagers on a motorbike.

One cigarette after another; it got to be eleven-fifteen. The transvestite disappeared, as did the two teenagers. An off-road vehicle carrying four loutish-looking kids approached. They shouted an obscene phrase at him. Diego merely gave them a look: they were silenced and took off, tires screeching. It wasn't clear even to him what the hell they had read in his look. He hadn't put anything into it, because at that moment he didn't exist; someone else was waiting in his place. But it had worked. Then out of nowhere an old Fiat 131 emerged. It proceeded uncertainly, a single headlight shining. Inside was Zaira. Diego took the seat beside her and she turned right, onto Via dei Laghi, in the direction of Velletri.

She was dressed in black and wore thick dark glasses. To Diego it seemed a bad omen. Her features shone with an unnatural pallor. She seemed depressed, suddenly aged. Diego circled her shoulders in a sort of affectionate and sympathetic embrace. He felt her stiffen.

"It was you, last night, right? With those men who were beating me up . . . "

"Leave me alone, don't say anything. I shouldn't be here with you now. I was just trying to get myself out of this damn business."

"How is he?"

"I don't know. I couldn't find him."

"What do you mean?"

"We had a telephone appointment. But he didn't answer."

"What do you think?"

"That it's over."

Diego took off the glasses. There were violet marks around her eyes.

"Is that my fault?"

Zaira didn't answer. Diego caressed her hair. He had never considered her anything more than a means of communication between him and Walid. And, in the beginning, her appearance on the scene had annoyed him. But there was real suffering in her. And that desperation couldn't be just an act.

"I'm sorry," he murmured, and lit a cigarette for her.

They went along Via dei Laghi for ten or maybe fifteen kilometers, until Zaira turned onto an unpaved road, and stopped with a jerk at the foot of a large tree.

"We're there?" he asked. An unnatural calm had taken possession of him. Zaira nodded.

They got out of the 131. The road ended in an expanse of dry leaves. An embryonic moon was peeking out of the dark. Zaira had a pocket flashlight. They continued, uphill, to a space that surrounded an apparently deserted cottage.

"There."

Diego took the flashlight and headed decisively toward the cottage. After a few steps, he realized that Zaira wasn't following him. He turned. She looked petrified, hands at her mouth, an expression of horror emanating from her tall figure, her head turned to a precise point, low down, on the left.

Diego aimed the flashlight at that point. He saw something move, rustling, in the dense brush, and heard a deep, mournful howl. A black shape darted away, an animal ran between the two of them, shooting into the darkness.

There was something on the ground. A body. Zaira was beside it. Diego bent down. It was the remains of something that must once have been a man. The outlines of a figure that had been agile, muscular could be guessed at. Shreds of a white raincoat, an arm twisted into an unnatural position, the flesh laid bare by vicious fangs. Traces of a recent fire, odor of gas. Diego stood up. He would never forget that fleshless void in place of the face. Zaira had moved a few steps away. Shaken by a violent, uninterrupted sob. He went over to her.

"Is it him?"

Zaira was weeping. Diego felt alone. Alone with himself and with that poor horrible thing. Was that the end of the line? Even the moon had averted its gaze from the grim scene. A thick drizzle had begun to fall again. He thought of Yusuf. Now it was up to him to take care of the little monster. Now that his first father was no longer there.

"We have to bury him."

The thought crossed his mind, like lightning, imperative. He went back to the body. He noticed a different odor, wild, pungent. A new rustling. The beast must have returned, he felt its hungry presence. The body had to be protected from that threatening presence. That was what had to be done. Diego began to dig in the wet earth with his bare hands, but there was a tangle of roots and the soft layer soon ended. His fingers touched something metal. A suitcase. He opened it mechanically. It was full of money. Dollars, pounds, bundles of brand-new banknotes in tidy piles, arranged one on top of the other, in observance of some comical geometry. Was it all because of this damn money, then? Wouldn't it be right to burn it, there, at that very moment? The echo of voices reached them.

Diego grabbed the suitcase and hurled himself toward Zaira.

"We have to get out of here!"

They began running away from the cottage. The voices were coming toward them. Flashes of light searched the darkness. He heard a dog bark. They threw themselves on the ground, in the shelter of a big tree trunk. A group of men passed by, almost touching them. Diego recognized Santini, panting, his face pale. The men headed toward the corpse. He saw Santini bend over, then something black appeared out of the darkness. A gigantic dog, a mad beast, planted itself to guard its prey, growling fiercely. Its jaws were open, drooling.

Zaira tried to pull him away, but Diego couldn't tear his eyes from the scene. He saw Santini waving something, a pistol, he saw the flash before hearing the sharp crack of the explosion, the dog barked and fell on one side, and its cries were extinguished in a faint, tormented wail. Santini took aim and gave the beast a death blow. Then he returned to Walid's body, shaking his head. He gave the gun to one of his men, and took from him a flashlight. He pointed it in the direction of the trees, very close to where Diego was hiding, and shouted a brief phrase:

"Marini! I know you're listening to me. You have shed this blood!"

Diego realized that Zaira had disappeared, and, in the grip of panic, began crawling until he reached the path and then the road. He ran and ran, until a truck driver, taking pity, picked him up and gave him a ride, dropping him near the abandoned factory. He got in his car and at the first light of dawn was at his in-laws' house. Only then did he notice, on the back seat of the car, the suitcase.

Chapter 20

Eight long months had passed since that night. There had been no news from either Zaira or the Major. Diego had tried to reassemble the fragments of his existence. He and Elsa had come very close to a definitive separation, but then, little by little, things got back to where they had been before: without his doing or explaining anything. He limited himself to asking her forgiveness, offering to let her go free and take the child himself. They had ended up in each other's arms at the height of an intense scene during which Diego hadn't opened his mouth. He spoke very little these days, because almost all the words that were said, by whomever said them, seemed to him useless or damaging.

If he thought over the events of that night, of his strange adventure, it seemed to him that he had been living a long dream: from time to time, when the memory of the facts became dangerously faint and doubt of their reality was about to prevail, he went to the cellar, lifted an old floor board, and took out the suitcase. He began to count the money: in all, between dollars, pounds, and Swiss francs, the equivalent of four hundred and fifty million lire. That damned money was the only tangible proof. And if he had decided to keep it, if he had resisted the temptation to spend it for himself (and God alone knew how he needed it!) or to give it to Santini, it was only because by right that money belonged to Yusuf. And if there was no way to get it to him, well then, he would burn it.

He alone was responsible for the death of Walid. It was a weight that he would carry with him all his life. But he had no intention of being overcome by despair. There were many important things to arrange, before declaring bankruptcy. Saving that money was all he could do to prove himself a worthy father for Yusuf; in the meantime he would be, for Giacomo, a different and better father. In those months he had begun to spend all his free moments with his son. He had learned to love him: he was no longer ashamed of him or of himself, and, what counted more, he was completely indifferent to the pity or annoyance of other people. Between him and Giacomo a tender confidence had been created that filled Elsa's heart with joy. And they had begun again to make love.

"You've changed," she said, afterward. He would have liked to answer that he deserved no credit for that. But every explanation would have been useless and damaging.

One evening in January they entrusted the child to a babysitter and went out to dinner. Elsa said she wanted another child. Diego said he would think about it.

"It's important."

He was on the point of telling her that they already had another child, only that because of him he was lost. But he was silent that time, too. A bitter sadness again fell upon them. They went home before eleven and he slept in the living room. At midnight the telephone rang. Diego was awake. He grabbed the receiver and whispered a tired "Hello?"

"Hello, my friend! Do you recognize me? No names."

Diego felt something melting inside him, and a surge of tears clouded his sight. It was Walid.

"I need your help . . . Are you listening?"

"Yes."

"In five minutes go to the telephone booth near your door. If it's occupied, get rid of whoever's inside. And wait for my call."

"Yes."

He got the suitcase. He did as he had been told. He waited anxiously in the phone booth for five minutes, then, finally, came the dull ring. Walid gave him rapid instructions. Diego took his car and went to a bar in the center of the city. He asked for Ali, and the bartender was pointed out to him, a thin, mean-looking Arab. He uttered an agreed-upon phrase, and Ali handed him a small woman's purse. Diego got back in the car and half an hour later parked in the service area at the Roma-Nord toll plaza, beside a taxi bearing the legend "Lima 16." Leaning on the taxi was a man in a billed cap smoking a cigarette. It was Walid.

They embraced, overcome by emotion. They couldn't find the right words. They didn't waste any useless or damaging ones. Walid was thinner, wrapped in a greasy overcoat, his hair long, but his gaze was clear, his smile gentle. Diego got in the taxi, Walid behind the wheel. They took the autostrada north toward Florence. For a while all they did was smoke one cigarette after another, then Walid broke the silence.

"I owe you some explanations, friend."

"I don't want to know anything."

"Maybe it's better that way."

In Prato it began to rain. The road was slippery and dangerous. The radio said there were fog banks beyond Piacenza. Diego shook off the torpor that had invaded him.

"How is Yusuf?"

Walid sighed.

"He's gone."

Diego gripped his friend's arm tight. "The party was for him, right?"

Walid nodded. "I knew you would understand," he said.

It was then that he had decided to change his life, had burned the bridges to his past.

"Now he's running, where space and time don't exist, and . . . "

He would have liked to console him, but words were only misery. He offered to drive, but Walid said that it was his job. Diego slipped into a heavy, dreamless sleep. When his friend woke him, he was happy to be beside him and he smiled. The car had stopped in a clear dawn.

"There is Ventimiglia, and then France. You get out here, Diego. I don't have the right to ask more of you."

"What happens if I get out?"

"Well, a taxi-driver with a passenger has a better chance of making it."

"Then let's go."

Walid searched in the woman's purse and took out a passport. The space for the photograph was empty. He stuck a photograph of himself in the square and signed with a scribble along the dotted line. They started off again. At the border there was a long line of trucks. The first light of day was burning off the fog. When it was their turn, and the guard, machine gun over his shoulder, took the documents, Walid nervously lit a cigarette. Diego handed over his Ministry I.D.. The guard gave back the documents. He was about to let them continue when his attention was caught by the suitcase.

"What's in there?"

Diego answered promptly, "Four hundred and fifty million in dollars and sterling."

The guard said something in dialect, laughed, and signaled them to go on.

They had breakfast in Mentone, in a small café that smelled of croissants and coffee. Diego had brought the suitcase with him.

"What will you do now, Walid?"

"I have an appointment with someone who owes me something. Then there will be another car, then a ship, and then . . . *Inshallah*, we are in the hands of the Lord."

"Someday or other we should talk about that again. About the Lord, I mean."

"It's not worth it, my friend. I've given up trying to understand."

"Then, see you again."

"See you again."

They shook hands. Walid gave a semblance of one of his usual smiles, and they embraced.

"I'll come see you someday. Now you have to think of your son. You were a good father to Yusuf. I'll try to be the same for Giacomo."

"This belongs to you," said Diego, offering him the suitcase.

Walid burst out laughing.

"So inside there really is . . . you must be mad! You took it! Well, you can keep it. It's no use to me."

"They're looking for you. You'll need it."

"Where I'm going no one looks for anyone, friend. It's another life."

"But it's yours . . . I've kept it all these months for Yusuf . . . "

Walid shook his head.

"Diego, Diego . . . If we still had tears . . . You keep that money. It will be useful to you, you'll see."

Half an hour later, at the station, as the departure of the train for Genoa was announced, Diego said to himself that, yet again, Walid had been right.

The money would be useful, very useful: but not for him, for his son. The one he would have with Elsa as soon as he got back to Rome. The one that would be born plump, smiling, and healthy. The one that was already waiting somewhere on the dark side of the universe, the son who had the right to all the happiness that had been denied to the other two and their fathers.

He wanted a boy, to call him Yusuf.

Giancarlo De Cataldo lives in Rome. A novelist, essayist, and television screenwriter, he is also a judge in the Court of Assizes in Rome. His books include *Black Like the Heart*, which inspired a film directed by Giancarlo Giannini, *Tender Assassins*, and *Criminal Tale*, which was recently made into a successful film by Michele Placido and featured at the Tribeca Film Festival.

Carmine Abate
Between Two Seas
"Abate populates this magical novel with a cast of captivating, emotionally complex characters."—*Publishers Weekly*
224 pp • $14.95 • ISBN: 978-1-933372-40-2

Stefano Benni
Margherita Dolce Vita
"A modern fable...hilarious social commentary."—*People*
240 pp • $14.95 • ISBN: 978-1-933372-20-4

Timeskipper
"Thanks to Benni we have a renewed appreciation
of the imagination's ability to free us from our increasingly mundane
surroundings."—*The New York Times*
400 pp • $16.95 • ISBN: 978-1-933372-44-0

Massimo Carlotto
The Goodbye Kiss
"A masterpiece of Italian noir."—*Globe and Mail*
160 pp • $14.95 • ISBN: 978-1-933372-05-1

Death's Dark Abyss
"A remarkable study of corruption and redemption
in a world where revenge is best served ice-cold."
—*Kirkus* (starred review)
160 pp • $14.95 • ISBN: 978-1-933372-18-1

The Fugitive
"The reigning king of Mediterranean noir."
—*The Boston Phoenix*
176 pp • $14.95 • ISBN: 978-1-933372-25-9

Steve Erickson
Zeroville
"A funny, disturbing, daring and demanding novel—Erickson's
best."—*The New York Times*
352 pp • $14.95 • ISBN: 978-1-933372-39-6

Elena Ferrante
The Days of Abandonment
"The raging, torrential voice of [this] author
is something rare."—*The New York Times*
192 pp • $14.95 • ISBN: 978-1-933372-00-6

Troubling Love
"Ferrante's polished language belies the rawness of her imagery,
which conveys perversity, violence, and bodily functions in ripe
detail."—*The New Yorker*
144 pp • $14.95 • ISBN: 978-1-933372-16-7

The Lost Daughter
"A resounding success . . . Delicate yet daring, precise
yet evanescent: it hurts like a cut, and cures like balm."
—*La Repubblica*
144 pp • $14.95 • ISBN: 978-1-933372-42-6

Jane Gardam
Old Filth
"Gardam's novel is an anthology of such bittersweet scenes, rendered by a novelist at the very top of her form."
—*The New York Times*
304 pp • $14.95 • ISBN: 978-1-933372-13-6

The Queen of the Tambourine
"This is a truly superb and moving novel."
—*The Boston Globe*
272 pp • $14.95 • ISBN: 978-1-933372-36-5

The People on Privilege Hill
"Artful, perfectly judged shifts of mood fill *The People on Privilege Hill* with an abiding sense of joy."—*The Guardian*
208 pp • $15.95 • ISBN: 978-1-933372-56-3

Alicia Giménez-Bartlett
Dog Day
"Delicado and Garzón prove to be one of the more engaging sleuth teams to debut in a long time."—*The Washington Post*
320 pp • $14.95 • ISBN: 978-1-933372-14-3

Prime Time Suspect
"A gripping police procedural."—*The Washington Post*
320 pp • $14.95 • ISBN: 978-1-933372-31-0

Death Rites
304 pp • $16.95 • ISBN: 978-1-933372-54-9

Katharina Hacker
The Have-Nots
"Hacker's prose, aided by Atkins's pristine translation, soars [as] she admirably explores modern urban life from the unsettled haves to the desperate have-nots."—*Publishers Weekly*
352 pp • $14.95 • ISBN: 978-1-933372-41-9

Patrick Hamilton
Hangover Square
"Hamilton is a sort of urban Thomas Hardy: always a pleasure to read, and as social historian he is unparalleled."
—Nick Hornby
336 pp • $14.95 • ISBN: 978-1-933372-06-8

James Hamilton-Paterson
Cooking with Fernet Branca
"Irresistible!"—*The Washington Post*
288 pp • $14.95 • ISBN: 978-1-933372-01-3

Amazing Disgrace
"It's loads of fun, light and dazzling as a peacock feather."
—*New York Magazine*
352 pp • $14.95 • ISBN: 978-1-933372-19-8

Alfred Hayes
The Girl on the Via Flaminia
"Immensely readable."—*The New York Times*
160 pp • $14.95 • ISBN: 978-1-933372-24-2

Jean-Claude Izzo
Total Chaos
"Izzo's Marseilles is ravishing. Every street, cafe
and house has its own character."—*Globe and Mail*
256 pp • $14.95 • ISBN: 978-1-933372-04-4

Chourmo
"A bitter, sad and tender salute to a place equally
impossible to love or to leave."—*Kirkus* (starred review)
256 pp • $14.95 • ISBN: 978-1-933372-17-4

Solea
"[Izzo is] a talented writer who draws from the deep,
dark well of noir."—*The Washington Post*
208 pp • $14.95 • ISBN: 978-1-933372-30-3

The Lost Sailors
"Izzo digs deep into what makes men weep."
—*Time Out New York*
272 pp • $14.95 • ISBN: 978-1-933372-35-8

A Sun for the Dying
"Beautiful, like a black sun, tragic and desperate."—*Le Point*
224 pp • $15.00 • ISBN: 978-1-933372-59-4

Gail Jones
Sorry
"In deft and vivid prose...Jones's gift for conjuring place
and mood rarely falters."—*Times Literary Supplement*
240 pp • $15.95 • ISBN: 978-1-933372-55-6

Matthew F. Jones
Boot Tracks
"I haven't read something that made me empathize with
a bad guy this intensely since I read *In Cold Blood*."
—*The Philadelphia Inquirer*
208 pp • $14.95 • ISBN: 978-1-933372-11-2

Ioanna Karystiani
The Jasmine Isle
"A modern Greek tragedy about love foredoomed, family
life as battlefield, [and] the wisdom and wantonness
of the human heart."—*Kirkus*
288 pp • $14.95 • ISBN: 978-1-933372-10-5

Gene Kerrigan
The Midnight Choir
"The lethal precision of his closing punches leave
quite a lasting mark."—*Entertainment Weekly*
368 pp • $14.95 • ISBN: 978-1-933372-26-6

Little Criminals
"A great story...relentless and brilliant."—Roddy Doyle
352 pp • $16.95 • ISBN: 978-1-933372-43-3

Peter Kocan
Fresh Fields
"A stark, harrowing, yet deeply courageous work
of immense power and magnitude."—*Quadrant*
304 pp • $14.95 • ISBN: 978-1-933372-29-7

The Treatment and The Cure
"A little masterpiece, not only in the history of prison
literature, but in that of literature itself."—*The Bulletin*
256 pp • $15.95 • ISBN: 978-1-933372-45-7

Helmut Krausser
Eros
"Helmut Krausser has succeeded in writing a great
German epochal novel."—*Focus*
352 pp • $16.95 • ISBN: 978-1-933372-58-7

Carlo Lucarelli
Carte Blanche
"Lucarelli proves that the dark and sinister
are better evoked when one opts for unadulterated
grit and grime."—*The San Diego Union-Tribune*
128 pp • $14.95 • ISBN: 978-1-933372-15-0

The Damned Season
"One of the more interesting figures
in crime fiction."—*The Philadelphia Inquirer*
128 pp • $14.95 • ISBN: 978-1-933372-27-3

Via delle Oche
"Lucarelli never loses his perspective on human nature
and its frailties."—*The Guardian*
160 pp • $14.95 • ISBN: 978-1-933372-53-2

Edna Mazya
Love Burns
"Combines the suspense of a murder mystery with
the absurdity of a Woody Allen movie."—*Kirkus*
224 pp • $14.95 • ISBN: 978-1-933372-08-2

Sélim Nassib
I Loved You for Your Voice
"Nassib spins a rhapsodic narrative out of the indissoluble
connection between two creative souls inextricably
bound by their art."—*Kirkus*
272 pp • $14.95 • ISBN: 978-1-933372-07-5

The Palestinian Lover
"A delicate, passionate novel in which history and
life are inextricably entwined."—*RAI Books*
192 pp • $14.95 • ISBN: 978-1-933372-23-5

Alessandro Piperno
The Worst Intentions
"A coruscating mixture of satire, family epic, Proustian
meditation, and erotomaniacal farce."—*The New Yorker*
320 pp • $14.95 • ISBN: 978-1-933372-33-4

Benjamin Tammuz
Minotaur
"A novel about the expectations and compromises that humans cre-
ate for themselves...Very much in the manner of William Faulkner
and Lawrence Durrell."—*The New York Times*
192 pp • $14.95 • ISBN: 978-1-933372-02-0

Chad Taylor
Departure Lounge
"There's so much pleasure and bafflement to be derived from
this thriller by novelist Chad Taylor."—*The Chicago Tribune*
176 pp • $14.95 • ISBN: 978-1-933372-09-9

Roma Tearne
Mosquito
"A lovely, vividly described novel."—*The Times* (London)
352 pp • $16.95 • ISBN: 978-1-933372-57-0

Christa Wolf
One Day a Year
"This remarkable book offers insight into the mind behind
the public figure."— *The New Yorker*
640 pp • $16.95 • ISBN: 978-1-933372-22-8

Edwin M. Yoder Jr.
Lions at Lamb House
"Yoder writes with such wonderful manners, learning,
and detachment."—William F. Buckley Jr.
256 pp • $14.95 • ISBN: 978-1-933372-34-1

Michele Zackheim
Broken Colors
"A profoundly original, beautifully written work, so emotionally
accurate that it tears at the heart. I read it without stopping."
—Gerald Stern
320 pp • $14.95 • ISBN: 978-1-933372-37-2

Children's Illustrated Fiction

Altan
Here Comes Timpa
48 pp • $14.95 • ISBN: 978-1-933372-28-0

Timpa Goes to the Sea
48 pp • $14.95 • ISBN: 978-1-933372-32-7

Fairy Tale Timpa
48 pp • $14.95 • ISBN: 978-1-933372-38-9

Wolf Erlbruch
The Big Question
52 pp • $14.95 • ISBN: 978-1-933372-03-7

The Miracle of the Bears
32 pp • $14.95 • ISBN: 978-1-933372-21-1

(with **Gioconda Belli**)
The Butterfly Workshop
40 pp • $14.95 • ISBN: 978-1-933372-12-9